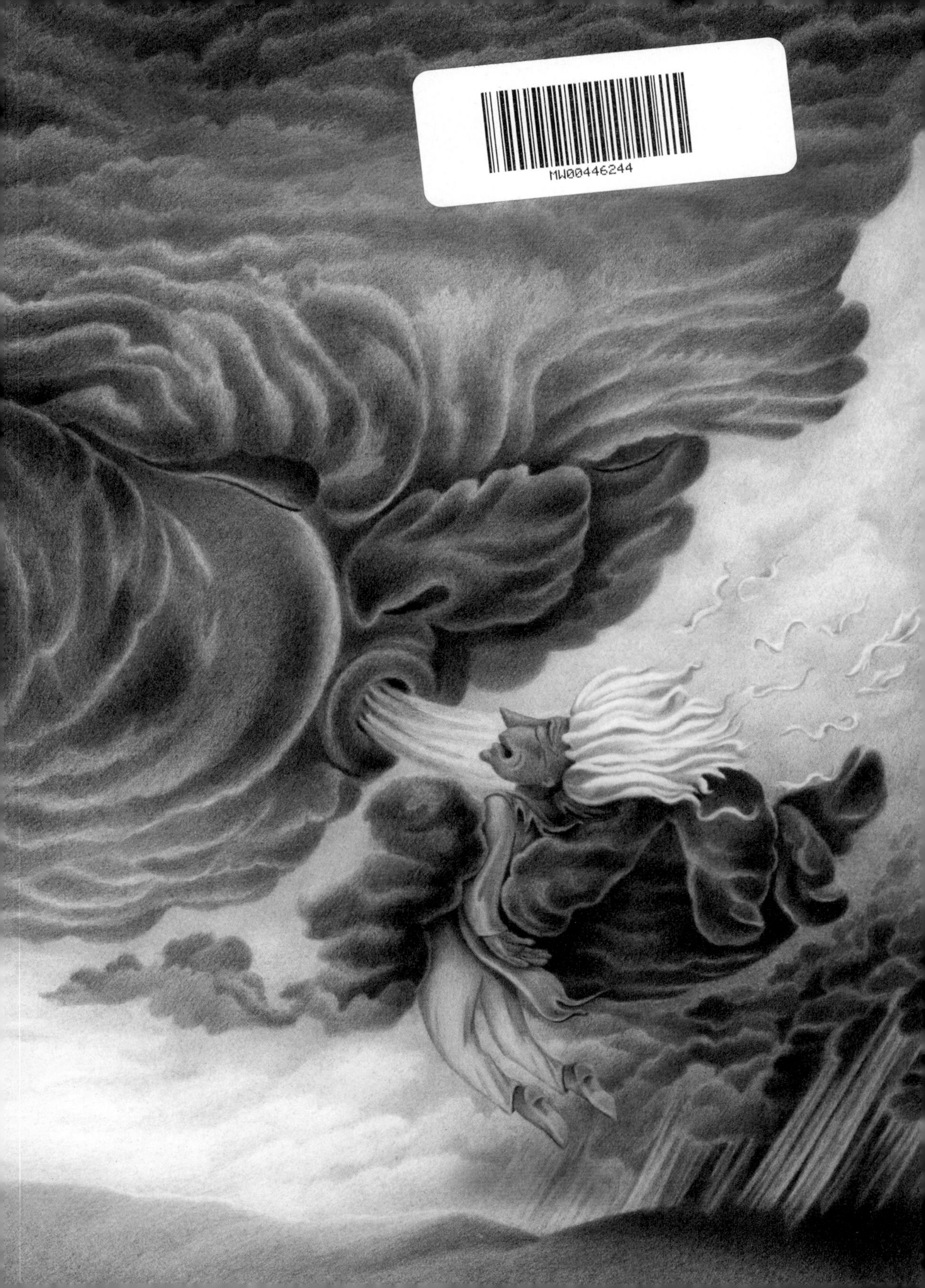

TUMBO
in The Shadows

✳ WRITTEN AND ILLUSTRATED BY ✳

Esther Samuels-Davis

〜

Tumbo in the Shadows
Written and illustrated by Esther Samuels-Davis
Edited by Emily Pollak, Laureen Mahler, and Roy Freeman
©2022 taotime books

Book design: Esther Samuels-Davis
Layout editing: Laureen Mahler
Fonts: Josefin Slab, La Belle Aurore, Philosopher, Monotype Sorts,
    Rambut Kusut, and Kelvinch

ISBN: 978-3-906945-29-3

taotime books
Thorenbergmatte 8
6014 Lucerne
Switzerland

taotimebooks.com
dirtyliketheweeds.com

Printed by Opolgraf, Poland

Dedicated to all of the journeys we've taken through Shadowland

T A B L E   O F

CONTENTS

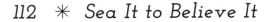

CHAPTER ONE

✳ A FINAL WISH ✳

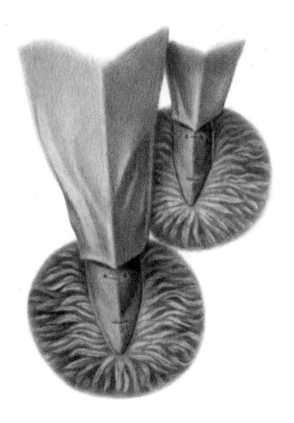

Gracefully, Tumbo made his way through the field. He placed each step with such poise that the blades of grass bowed down beside his green leather shoes. He smiled with the calm confidence he had been taught to embody: the lines around his mouth creasing just right, the wrinkles by his eyes like radiant sparks firing out from his lashes.

Tumbo was ready. He had spent his life preparing for tomorrow morning's audition, and now, on the evening before his one hundred-and-fifth birthday, he would savor these last moments of youth.

Reaching the edge of the wood, Tumbo stopped to reflect beneath his favorite birch tree. This tree had grown apart from the rest of the grove. It stood alone, as if it was on a stage preforming for the grasses of the field. Tomorrow morning, he would be like this tree, in front of the jury in Terra Floss. Tumbo sat down beneath the birch, resting his precious white curls carefully on its trunk. He closed his eyes and took a deep breath.

Oh this wondrous hair! thought Tumbo. It was thanks to these curls that he could even *consider* trying out for the Drifting Dandys. He'd gone through the requirements so many times, Tumbo could practically see them scrolled onto the backs of his eyelids.

Drifting Dandy Qualifications:

1. Minimum age of one hundred and five

2. Joyful wrinkles only

3. 30 years of training at a performing arts university

4. Master's degree in Wish Granting

5. MOST Important: A full head of white curls

A Terra Flossian would be hard pressed to name an honor higher than becoming one of the Drifting Dandys. Each year the traveling troupe visited all the towns and cities of the province, granting one wish to every person who asked.

Tumbo closed his eyes, remembering how the Dandys paraded into his village each spring. He recalled how the townsfolk would form a line in the city center, and one by one present their wish to a Dandy. The Dandy would listen closely and pluck out one of their very own curly white hairs with great care.

Holding the hair between thumb and forefinger, they would perform a series of special movements that were needed for that particular wish to come true, then blow the hair up into the sky.

With his eyes still closed, Tumbo went over his wish-granting drills. Though being born with wish-granting hair was a matter of luck, learning to perform the particular movements correctly took years of practice. These motions were important, as they filled the hair with the power it needed for a person's wish to come true.

After decades of training, Tumbo couldn't have been more ready for his life's work to begin. His heart fluttered in anticipation. He looked down into the grass beside him for comfort.

Well, what do you know? he thought. *A ripe old dandelion just asking to be wished upon! The Terra Flossian's way to wish when there is no Dandy to help them.* Tumbo looked down at the flower and thought back to his studies. *Dandelion seeds are not always as accurate as a Dandy's hair, but what do I have to lose, my life's purpose will commence tomorrow!*

Snatching it up, Tumbo closed his eyes and sparked his smile. "I wish to be the most exceptional wish granter

Terra Floss has ever seen!" He took a deep breath and blew his final wish into the wind. A moment passed, and there was... a rumble. Tumbo opened his eyes with a start—wishing was normally a silent practice. He looked up to the sky, which in a moment had turned from a happy blue into murky gray. Tumbo brought his hands to his mouth—it couldn't be! Marching right towards him was a plump, menacing thundercloud. At the rate it was traveling, it would soon be right on top of him!

"Flower saints preserve us, I can't have the rain ruin my hair right before try-outs!" he cried.

Tumbo's heart pounded. The hairdresser had done such a lovely job primping and preening his curls earlier that morning. It was an extra-special hairdo for the audition, *and it could not get wet.* He would have to make a run for it. The thundercloud rumbled again, hovering between him and Terra Floss.

If I go at top speed I can pass underneath before it starts to storm, he thought.

Without a dry moment to spare, Tumbo sprang to his feet, dashing back through the field towards the oncoming thundercloud, and the direction of home.

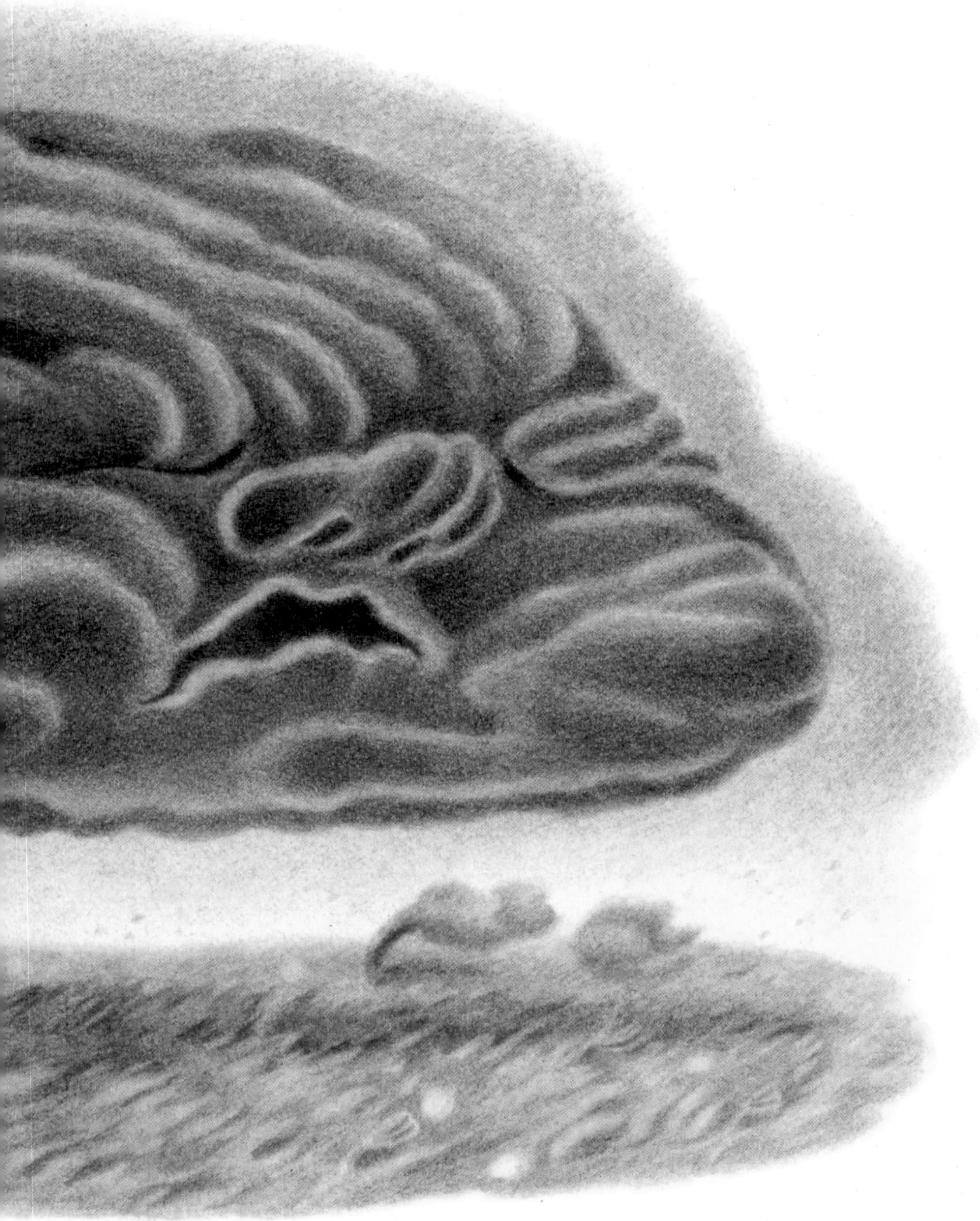

CHAPTER TWO

✳ THE THING ABOUT THUNDERCLOUDS ✳

Calling upon the early days of his training when he'd learned ballet, Tumbo raced over the grass in an effortless series of split leaps. At a glance he could have been flying. But to his dismay, the gloomy cloud was charging ever still, right for him. Tumbo feared for the worst.

"If roses are red, please keep dry my head!" Tumbo prayed in panic as he sprang through the grass.

High in the sky, Gerald the thundercloud was very upset. Contrary to what many may assume, thunderclouds do not like confrontations, *especially* with other clouds. Their temperamental demeanor may appear threatening, but it's only a defense. Thunderclouds are in fact a highly sensitive sort of cloud, and Gerald, flying home from a hard day at Sky School, was on the verge of a downpour.

"Someday I'll give those rain squeezers a taste of their own medicine..." Gerald grumbled as he stormed over the field. "Next time they tease me I won't fly away like a coward... from this point on, no more Mr. Nice Cloud!"

Unbeknownst to Tumbo, from a cloud's perspective his body was completely hidden underneath his billowing white curls. Looking down, Tumbo appeared like a giant ball of fluff hurdling over the grass. Gerald spied him advancing below, and right away mistook him for yet *another* bully swooping in to tease him. The merciless taunts by the clouds that day at Sky School still rang in his ears. Gerald held fast to his new identity as a tough cloud and tried to remain strong.

He began to rumble and quake in panic. "Don't you come any closer, you hear me?! Keep away... or... I'll strike!"

But down on the ground Tumbo kept on running. If anything, he scampered even faster now because of Gerald's shouting—which, of course, sounded like plain old thunder to Tumbo.

"Cloud heavens above!" Gerald boomed. "Stay back, I say! Back! Well... you asked for it!!" The storm cloud closed his eyes and shot down a warning bolt. His first bold act of self-defense.

Silence. Gerald blew out a sigh of relief and looked around for the retreating cumulus. But the puffy little cloud was nowhere to be seen. *Oh no,* he thought. *Oh no oh no oh no... Have I... have I vaporized them?*

Gerald scanned the sky in desperation. Indeed, there was no trace of the cloud. But as he peered down into the field where the bully had been, he noticed something in the grass that had certainly not been there seconds earlier: a wrinkled hairless creature in a little green suit, not moving a muscle.

To call Tumbo hairless wasn't entirely accurate. Perhaps from a cloud's perspective it appeared so, but in actuality there were still three very tenacious hairs stubbornly clinging to each side of Tumbo's head. Six hairs in total.

He lay sprawled out over the scorched earth in shock.

What ... had ... just ... happened? Tumbo couldn't manage to think a thought. Of course, he hadn't seen what the thundercloud had seen—Tumbo wasn't aware how threatening he had appeared. Last he knew, he had been running through a field to escape rain, and now he found himself flat on his back, body quivering against the ground.

As Tumbo's senses slowly returned, he could smell a faint smoldering aroma. *How curious...* he thought.

The *pat pat* of raindrops began to hit his cheeks. Still grasping the mission of protecting his curly locks (may they rest in peace), Tumbo instinctively brought his arms up to his head to shield them. Poor Tumbo. Poor, poor Tumbo. It was at this point that any innocent bystander would have wanted to cover their ears, for the soil-smashing, rock-crushing, grass-splitting shriek that emerged from Tumbo's lips was filled with such anguish that Gerald fled in horror.

Tumbo's hands searched frantically over and around the top of his head like delirious explorers lost in a snowstorm. What was this new terrain, as bare as tundra? Where were his luscious curls? It took Tumbo more than a moment to fully comprehend his new reality. And when it had become clear, all he could do was lie with his knees against his chest and sob, hands tucked firmly under his chin. He couldn't bear to lay a finger on the strange phenomenon that now surrounded his perfectly wrinkled features.

"I have worked so deliberately on these wrinkles," wailed Tumbo. "I've always made sure to express only the happiest of expressions. These lines are a masterpiece, and now... and... now..."

Tumbo folded his legs in closer, clenching his hands to his coat in tight fists.

"All those decades of theater and dance, of *Wherefore art thous* and stupid pirouettes. And my degree in Wish Granting?! Years of training to learn each precise movement to make silly dreams come true. Might as well flush those right down the drain. Flush them away just like my fluffy white... Just like my flu... fy..."

Tumbo erupted into a tyrannosaurus tantrum of howls and tears.

"How can I ever show my head in Terra Floss again! A head so empty, so void of everything it could have been." Tumbo whimpered. "And my parents? It would simply break their honeysuckle hearts to see me... a failure. It's better they think I've blown away, like a tumbleweed."

There was no longer any point in going to the audition. When a Dandy gives a hair away as a wish, that hair will *never* grow back—not even if they use a hair to *wish* it back. That is why their wishes are so powerful, and a Dandy's hair so unique. With six wishes left to give and no possibility of growing new wishes, he wouldn't even be able to make it through a single town visit. At the audition tomorrow he would be laughed off stage and into oblivion.

CHAPTER THREE

✳ INTO OBLIVION ✳

Holding on to the six hairs of dignity that had been spared, Tumbo didn't go to the try-outs. He also didn't return to Terra Floss. What he did do, however, was remain lying right in that very field. For weeks. Flat on his back, he stared up into a cloudless sky. It was a beautiful blue, a color that only a month before would have provoked a classically contagious Tumbo smile, but now—nothing. His purpose, his life of training, gone in a flash. He lay lifeless, hoping for the grass to take him under.

Though Tumbo may have *felt* useless, that doesn't mean he *was* useless. In some worlds, having lost the will to move can actually be a rather desirable quality. Maybe not in the world in which Terra Floss existed, but lucky for Tumbo, Terra Floss was only in *one* world. Infinity is *full* of worlds. Some above, some below—and others right beside Tumbo and Terra Floss.

There are not many beings who are able to see into other worlds, but the ones who could rose to power quickly. In the world of Shadows, that being was Dog, the very first of his kind in Shadowland. In addition to having a different form, he was also the only shadow ever to be born with a sense of smell. With this unique ability, Dog had discovered other possibilities for the way shadows could live their lives. The moment he came to power, his voice was heard booming over the shadow landscape, barking ideas to his fellow shadows about a new way to be.

It had been thousands of years since that pivotal moment, but the words he called out that day were still remembered with reverence throughout Shadowland, especially during the solo season.

"At the beginning of time," Dog's voice had bellowed, "when all the worlds were created, each was

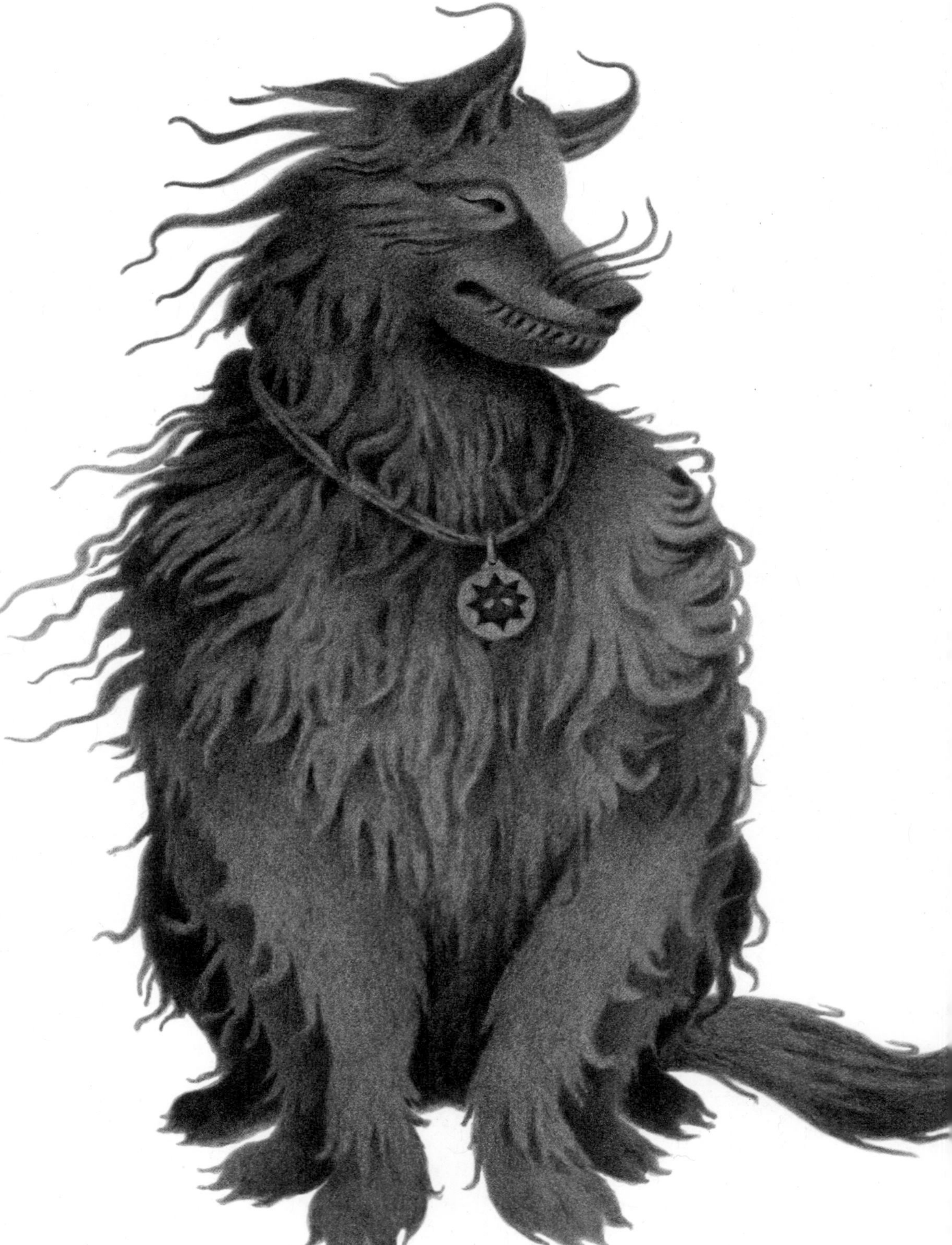

separate from the other. Each that is, except for Shadowland and the Land of Light. Somehow our worlds have remained attached, just at the very edges. As a result of this attachment, we shadows cannot exist without our light counterparts, and they cannot exist without us. Light needs shadow to be able to rest, and we shadows live from the energy that light beings generate. In our relationship with light, it has always felt natural to move when they move, to be where they are. It feels good to be together, they are true companions. But my dear shadows, what if I told you that we could exist on our own, *move* on our own—without light?"

The shadows listening that day had murmured in utter confusion.

"What if I told you," Dog continued, "that I have smelled something in Shadowland that we didn't know was here. My shadows, I am eager to tell you that there is food—shadow food that grows all around us! With no sense of smell, we never before knew it existed. But I, Dog, was born with the ability to smell—and I smelled something, I smelled *a lot* of things. Summoning all the strength my paws could muster, I reached out and grabbed some of this something... and I *ate* it. Then I stood up... entirely on my own."

There was a collective gasp from all the shadows in Shadowland.

"I know what you're thinking: it's not right to leave our companions unable to rest. Not to mention, we will certainly miss being separated from their energy. But even the best of friends can benefit from time spent apart. I'm sure that many of you would prefer to stay connected with your light companions most of the time, but I have an idea, one that will give you an opportunity to be apart for just a season each year."

Dog took a deep breath. "My shadows, I have found a way we can leave them, *only* temporarily, and they won't notice a thing. You see, the more I ate, the better my sense of smell grew, and now, I have developed an ability to smell into other worlds. What would you say if by using this skill, I could personally search out beings from the Land of Light who have lost all purpose in life. I can bring them here to Shadowland to work as temporary shadows for our companions. I can give purpose to Land of Light beings who have misplaced all hope. But most importantly, I, Dog, can give you a taste of what it feels like to be on your own. You will be able to experience our world in a whole new way, the way that I have been able to since discovering my ability. For the first time since the very beginning of our world, you, my dear shadows, can journey into Shadowland, and you can do it all by yourselves."

The shadows had erupted in jubilation. Their existence would be altered from that day forward.

For Dog, the optimism he had felt those thousands of years ago now seemed like another lifetime. The temp shadow system had worked wonders throughout the centuries. As shadows took time away from light, they were able to explore the depths of Shadowland, building their own cities and creating new and exciting ways to eat shadow food. But this year, there was a problem. Most of the temp hires that Dog had brought to Shadowland last year were lightbulbs, and they had turned out to be faulty.

It was late summer, the season when nearly every shadow traveled to Umbraton, the solo-time capitol of Shadowland. Dog would need to fill all their places, or else... no solo trips this year. Dog took such pride in his ability to see through to other worlds that he had never trained another shadow in the skill. Thus, for the last few thousand years, he was the only being who could find temp hires, and because of this year's problem, Dog was overwhelmed and exhausted.

Even after weeks of sniffing desperately throughout the Land of Light for beings who had lost all purpose, Dog *still* hadn't found enough hires for the season. Frantic, he ran faster, scampering clumsily over the landscape, until—"OOF." He tripped and fell. Dog buried his snout in his paws.

"Where have all the lost beings gone?" he whined.

He looked behind him to see what in the Land of Light he had tripped over. *A moss-covered stone? But no—it seems the stone is ... breathing?...* Dog stood and turned to investigate. He leaned his snout down next to the object to get a better sniff.

This is indeed no stone! At a closer glance, Dog saw that it was a smooth-headed creature dressed in a little green suit. Aside from the soft breathing that could be felt from its nose, the creature was completely motionless. *Definitely still alive but... barely.*

Dog sat up straight and grinned. *I cannot believe my luck,* he thought. *This one will be perfect!*

He got right to work, pawing for his reading glasses. "All right, let's see... where is that checklist?" Dog's voice echoed.

He fumbled around in his shadow fur, searching for the temp shadow paperwork. For someone who was good at finding things, Dog was *also* good at losing them.

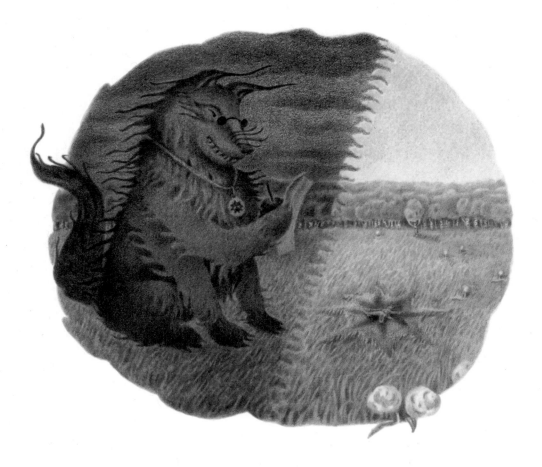

"Ah, bingo!" He pulled a crumpled-up paper from behind his ear and smoothed it with a paw. "Now what do we have here..." Dog cleared his throat. "Number one: Ability to lie still... check! Number two: Usable silhouette... a bit unusual, but someone at The Center will make it work, we found positions for all those lightbulbs after all... check! Number three: Complete loss of purpose..."

Dog paused.

"Well... it does seem wholly miserable. I would normally wait longer before recruiting a being but..."

Dog looked down, as if to inspect an imaginary watch. He huffed, running his tongue over sharp teeth. "I'm running out of time; it must be done." Dog reached into the field with his shimmery snout, picked up Tumbo by his little green coattails, and pulled him through into Shadowland.

CHAPTER FOUR

✳ AT THE CENTER ✳

Just like that, Tumbo was in the dark. Sensing that his legs were bent and there was a surface under the seat of his pants, he gathered he was sitting on some sort of chair. The darkness was so consuming that at first he thought his eyes were still closed, but after giving one of them a poke, he was sure. It was just very, very dark in here, or... out here, wherever he was. Surprisingly he didn't really care. Sitting on the chair, Tumbo didn't actually feel... anything. He wasn't hot or cold, he wasn't really sad, but he wasn't really happy either. It all felt like...

"Nothing... whatever *that* is," Tumbo muttered to himself aloud. He rolled his eyes. Now that he couldn't be a Drifting Dandy, he could make any rude expression his heart desired.

"Excuse me, hun. Do we already have an attitude problem here?"

Tumbo nearly fell out of his seat. Now *that* stirred a feeling in him. Being abruptly pulled into darkness was one thing, but an ominous voice in that darkness? He smoothed his coattails before sitting back down.

"I'm sorry, Ms. ... Mr. ..."

"You can call me Jerry," the voice replied curtly.

"Pardon me, Ms. Jerry, I hadn't realized there was anyone else... here."

"I said, 'Call me Jerry,'" the voice huffed.

Jerry tried to hide the sharp edge of annoyance in her tone. She knew these temp hires were disoriented—most had never even *heard* of Shadowland. But that didn't make it any less irritating every time she had to debrief them.

"It will take you a moment to adjust to the dark," Jerry droned. "But don't you worry, you will be able to see like you do in the Land of Light in no time."

"Land of Light?"

"You're in Shadowland," said Jerry. She sighed. "It's a world right next to yours. We call your world the Land of Light."

"There are other... worlds?" stammered Tumbo.

Jerry sighed again.

"Yes," she said impatiently. "Welcome to Shadowland. Well, to be specific, welcome to the Shadowland Job Placement Center. 'The Center' for short."

"Job Placement Center?" Tumbo never dreamed he would be qualified to hold any kind of position other than Drifting Dandy... and that was obviously no longer a possibility. "Do you mean... you're trying to find a job for... for me?"

There was a tinge of gratitude in those last few words. Sensing Tumbo's appreciation, Jerry softened.

"Well yes, Ms. ... Mr. ..." Jerry paused, realizing she had forgotten to give this new hire the sign-in sheet.

"Please, call me Tumbo."

"Well, Tumbo," Jerry continued, "you have been personally selected by Dog, the ruler of Shadowland, for the very honorable position of temp shadow hire."

"Selected personally by your ruler... for a position? So, I'm not... completely... useless?" he said with a slight smile.

"Every being can have a purpose in Shadowland," Jerry said, "as long as they follow the rule."

Tumbo couldn't believe it. The prospect of having a job was so thrilling he didn't even think twice about where in the worlds Shadowland was, or that there were whole different worlds outside of his own for that matter.

Tumbo felt a warm excitement rise up from his chest. His eyes *sparkled*.

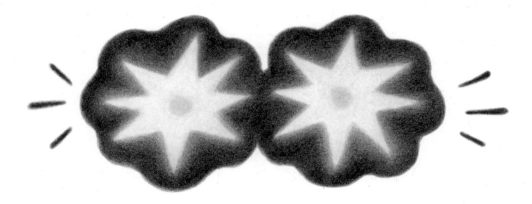

"WHOA there," cautioned Jerry. *Sheesh. Dog must really be desperate for hires to have let another sparker in,* Jerry thought to herself. "Tumbo, you MUST refrain from using any light down here."

"But I..."

"No light is EVER allowed, thank you. We can't have any sparks burning holes through the borders of Shadowland. Now... let's see... who could you match with..."

Tumbo heard the clickety-click of typing.

"Nope... nope... nunh-unh..." The clicking continued. "Wait a sec... yes. This old girl is too perfect. Dang it, Jerry, you've done it again."

Jerry's tone, though even, was as pleased as a prideful pat on the back.

As Tumbo's eyes adjusted to the darkness, forms in the room began to emerge. He could make out a figure sitting in front of a computer monitor. She was nodding to herself in satisfaction. Her shape undulated in the gloom, and he could see that she had a large bun tied up on top of her head. Tumbo felt tears gathering behind his eyes. *What a joy it would be to twist such a bun into being.*

Jerry made one final triumphant click with her mouse. The printer beside her squealed to life with beeps and boops, and in time spat out a piece of paper. She promptly handed it over the desk to Tumbo for his approval. Printed on the page was a black silhouette of...

Tumbo squinted, "Is that... me?" He looked up at Jerry. "Is this some kind of mockery?"

Jerry chuckled, "I did do a good job matching you, didn't I? No, Tumbo, this isn't you, meet Bonnie. Bonnie, the birch tree," she said. "You will be her shadow this fall. Lucky for you, trees are beings who know shadows are beings too. So you'll have someone to talk to."

Tumbo looked back down at the paper.

"The job is pretty straightforward," Jerry explained. "As a shadow, you will be continually attached to your Land of Light being, in your case, Bonnie. You will move when she moves, sleep when she sleeps, be where she is. Get the idea?"

Tumbo nodded.

"You are there to give her a little rest from all the energy in the Land of Light, got it?"

He nodded again.

"Besides shadowing, there is only one rule here in Shadowland: Stay put."

"Stay put?" Tumbo chuckled. "Well, that doesn't sound so challenging."

"It may sound easy, but it's important." Jerry straightened. "Shadowland is shaped like, well... like this." Jerry took out a pencil and drew two lines in the margin of Tumbo's printout. It looked to Tumbo like a capital "T." Jerry proceeded, "This top line here is where Shadowland overlaps with the Land of Light. That is where we shadows and you Land of Light beings live together. But Shadowland also extends far below the Land of Light." Jerry traced the vertical line of the "T" with her pencil. "In this part of Shadowland there is no connection to the Land of Light. This is a dangerous place for temp hires, it's easy for you to get lost. Forever. And we don't want any beings lost out there doing who knows what. So—stay put."

Tumbo nodded. "I surely don't need to be any more lost than I already am."

"That's what I like to hear," said Jerry. "To accept your position, I will just have you sign here on the dotted line."

Tumbo noticed a block of text underneath the image of Bonnie. It was no language he'd ever studied back at the Wish-Granting Academy in Terra Floss, but he *could* make out a dotted line in the center of other squiggly marks. Jerry handed him a pen that was attached to her desk by a chain. He took it, and with large curly letters, Tumbo signed.

Jerry clapped her wispy hands together. "Glad to have you on board Tumbo."

And with that, she stamped the piece of paper with a loud KA-CHING! and filed it away.

CHAPTER FIVE

✳ THE NOT-SO-BONNIE BIRCH TREE ✳

Once again, Tumbo was in a field. A very dark field. And not like the fields at night back in Terra Floss, no—this field seemed to be *made* of darkness itself.

Am I made of darkness as well?

Tumbo tried to raise an arm to inspect himself, but in doing so discovered he couldn't even move a finger.

Tumbo's heartbeat quickened. He tried to look around for help but found he couldn't turn his head. The only living being in his direct line of vision was a tree that grew at his feet. Or at least, the remnants of a tree.

Dandelions above, what's happened to this poor creature? thought Tumbo.

He squinted his eyes and realized that he recognized this shape; it was the one from the paper that Jerry had printed for him.

"Miss B-Bonnie?" Tumbo said shyly. Though he was very fond of birch trees, Tumbo had never actually talked to one. Back in Terra Floss they would have called him a madman for that, and what jury would ever let a madman into the Drifting Dandys? No matter. *Now* he could talk to any old tree he wanted.

Bonnie rustled what was left of her leaves. As she did, Tumbo sensed the six hairs on his head wiggling. He caught sight of one of them. Instead of being white, his hairs were now a transparent dark gray.

So this is shadowing, Tumbo thought.

"Are you my new understudy?" Bonnie's voice was soft and clear.

Tumbo caught his breath. *My daisies, Jerry wasn't lying—trees can talk to shadows...*

He took a second to compose himself.

"Jerry from The Center assigned me here," he said. "At least, she said I was assigned to a Miss Bonnie the birch tree. I assume you are she?"

The tree was silent for a few moments. "A new shadow? That's right, I'd forgotten that the solo season has begun. You have to pardon me, Ms. ... Mr. ..."

"Please feel free to call me Tumbo."

"My apologies, Tumbo, my memory hasn't been the same ever since I was cut through."

Bonnie let those last two words linger in the wind that whirled around her lost branches.

Cut through.

Tumbo could feel that her wounds were still fresh. *Or is it the wound from atop my own trunk that I am feeling?* Tumbo found it was hard to tell his senses apart from Bonnie's, now that he was her shadow.

"I can see that... that something happened to your trunk," Tumbo said cautiously.

"Yes," Bonnie creaked. "It *was* something. They wanted electricity in a new suburb of the city, and I am growing right in the path where the power lines were planned. The arborists were kind enough to spare my life, but in doing so they had to cut through my trunk. I must look so silly."

It was true; Bonnie didn't look nearly as handsome as Tumbo's beloved birch back home. Tumbo thought about his own silly silhouette. "You and me both, Bonnie. You and me both."

CHAPTER SIX

✳ MIRROR IMAGE ✳

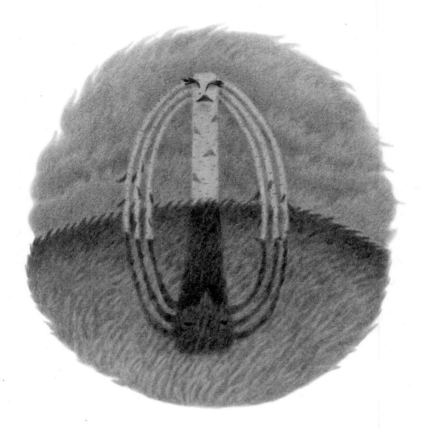

Days upon days of darkness passed by, and through them all Tumbo was only able to look at one thing: Bonnie. A perfect reflection of his own shattered hopes and dreams. Only in sleep was there a moment's rest from the reminder of his new form, that he too had been cut through, that his magnificent curls were gone for good. Minute by minute, Tumbo grew increasingly more bitter towards this creature to which he was bound.

How can she even stand to be around herself, looking like that? he thought.

Like Jerry had said, as Bonnie's shadow, Tumbo could only move when she moved, only be where she was. And since Bonnie was a tree, Tumbo couldn't go anywhere. With nothing to distract him, the memory of the thundercloud haunted his thoughts through every dark day.

Though moving was not an option, Tumbo *could* still speak. In his former life, theater class had been one of Tumbo's favorites. He took any chance he could get to tell a good story, or sing an old Flossian ballad... but now?

What can I sing of now? he thought. *I never want to recite the story of that treacherous thundercloud and its soul-splitting lightning bolt!*

Remembering the event felt like there were thorns tearing through his heart. To make matters worse, even if he had the will to tell the tragic tale, the only being there to listen was his own hideous doppelgänger.

Tumbo grew ever quieter as the weeks passed. He silently stewed over the loss of his curls, his anger rising towards his repulsive silhouette. He felt as raw and angry as a boiled egg.

Bonnie was used to her shadows being quiet, but she sensed a tension between herself and this new temp hire that made her uneasy. As time passed and her discomfort grew, Bonnie began to wonder. "Tumbo? I don't mean to intrude," her windy voice wavered, "but... is everything all right?"

Tumbo wanted to freeze and explode all at once. He chose the latter. "Pfff, as if talking to your pathetic excuse for a tree could help anything..."

Bonnie didn't move a leaf. Tumbo could sense the pain of his sharp words running down to her roots, but he didn't soften. "Your unsightly trunk reminds me every second of my waking shadow life that the future I was *supposed* to have has been completely and utterly destroyed!"

Bonnie stayed quiet, but her leaves looked like they were trying to hide themselves. Tumbo's six hairs curled tightly together. Every sour word he spoke bounced right back into his soul.

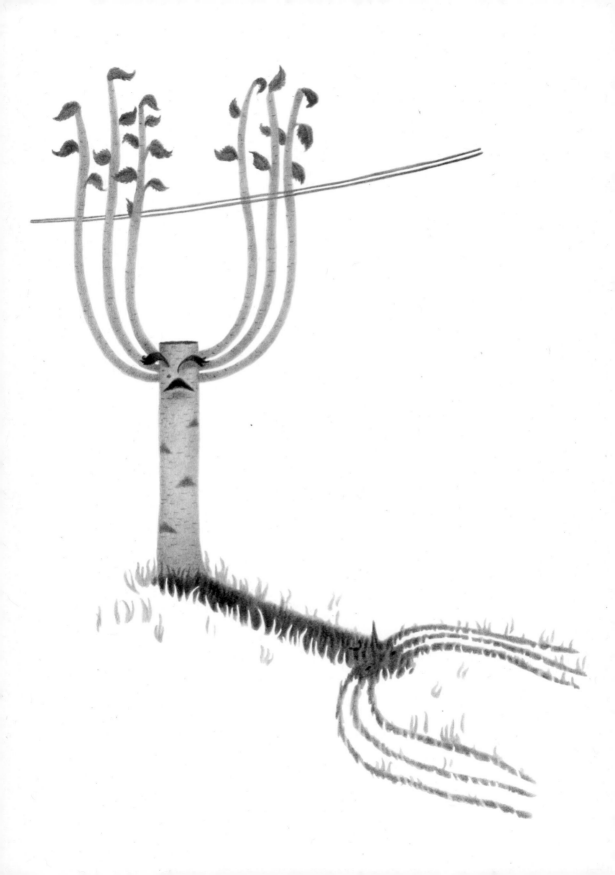

Flowers above, that really hurt. Tumbo clenched his teeth. The instant he had spoken the words aloud, he knew they were wrong to say.

"I'm... I'm sorry Bonnie. Really, I'm..."

Bonnie tried to turn away—and so did her shadow.

Tumbo quivered. *Who is this terrible beast I have become?* he thought. *Drifting Dandys are never supposed to lose their tempers.* Tumbo could feel the hurt in Bonnie's branches. *She's not at fault for what happened to her,* Tumbo realized. *Bonnie is the last being who deserves such an unfair attack.*

He was going to have to explain himself. Even if the story was painful to recount.

"My behavior has been unforgivable, Bonnie."

Bonnie remained silent.

"But I think I was really saying those poisonous things to... myself," Tumbo sighed. "Bonnie, I know I'm no tree, but I think I may understand how you feel. How *it* feels. To be cut through."

"How could you ever understand, Tumbo?" Bonnie's voice was small and splintery. "You can take any form you like after you shadow for me... but I'll be stuck like this forever, as long as these power lines remain here in the grove."

"The thing is, Bonnie, I'm not actually from around here." Tumbo paused, knowing she wouldn't be very thrilled to hear where he *was* from. "Before Shadowland... I used to be... well the kind of being who cut through your trunk... I am originally from the Land of Light."

He felt her branches run cold. Tumbo swore he could hear the six hairs on his head whispering to one another in terror. "Before you never speak to me again Bonnie, I extend my deepest apologies on behalf of my species. What happened to your trunk was truly ruthless."

She still said nothing, but he saw that his words had somewhat pacified her foliage, and in turn, his curls.

"And the way I look?" Tumbo continued. "Well, the shape of my shadow is the shape of myself... and always will be." Bonnie perked up. Tumbo went on, "Maybe I will start from the beginning... if that's all right with you?"

Bonnie bowed her trunk.

At least if I start from the beginning... I can ease into the hard part of the story, he thought.

Tumbo took a deep breath. "Long in the past, before my studies, before my childhood, before there was a me at all, my parents lived alone and childless in a meager hut woven from forsythia branches." He sighed. "Neither had grown up with much money, but they *had* grown up in large loving families. When my mother and father met, they dreamed of having many children together, just like the families in which they had been raised. Only, contrary to their parents before them, they were determined to grow rich. Alas, each passing year of their marriage grew more bitter than the last, as neither wealth nor children came to them. Their humble dandelion farm could barely make stems meet, and try as they might, they were unable to bear a child. But not all hope was lost, for in Terra Floss there is a famous group of traveling wish granters. They call themselves the Drifting Dandys."

Tumbo broke from the story.

"Have you heard of them?" he asked anxiously. Bonnie shook her leaves, no.

Tumbo exhaled. "Truly?"

Bonnie shook her leaves again.

Never even heard of the Dandys? Tumbo puzzled. "Well, no matter," he continued, "for this story, it is only important to know that in order to be a Drifting Dandy you need to have curly white hair."

He took another deep breath.

"And these hairs, along with a *lot* of training, are able to grant wishes. The Dandys travel throughout the province, and in every village, they stop to grant wishes to the townsfolk. My parents were desperate for a child, so when the Dandys arrived in their own small village, they simply couldn't resist. They made a wish, and months later out I came into the world, curls first. My parents had never seen a happier day in their lives. Not only did they have the child of whom they had dreamt, they also knew I had a bright future ahead of me, full of the prosperity they had always desired. For only those born with wish-granting curls can become Drifting Dandys."

Tumbo paused for dramatic effect, but then remembered that Bonnie had never even *heard* of the Dandys.

"Drifting Dandy happens to be the most respected position in all of Terra Floss," he clarified.

Bonnie let out an understanding "ooOOhh!"

Tumbo went on, recounting his days at the performing arts university and how he had later toiled through his wish-granting thesis. "I spent months bent over my desk, writing day and night. So unaware of my surroundings— the mountain of dirty buttercups from which I had drunk my pollen tea grew so tall that by the time I was finished it nearly touched the ceiling. But all my hard work felt worth it in the end. My parents couldn't have been prouder the day my thesis was approved."

Tumbo sighed. "I can't imagine what they would think of me now," he murmured to himself.

Bonnie softened. Never had she met such an intriguing shadow. At last, Tumbo came to the turning point of his tale. Bonnie's limbs quaked as he told of the lightning bolt, and by the end she reached out her branches to give Tumbo a hug. Being her shadow, Tumbo reached for Bonnie as well.

"I understand now why you had an outburst," said Bonnie. "I also understand how you understand *me*. I think it will be a pleasure to have you as a shadow, Tumbo."

Tumbo felt a warmth run through his shadow hairs.

The two spent the rest of the afternoon trading stories. Bonnie told him about her time as a sprout, fighting her way through the grasses, and later as a sapling, when she stayed awake past sunset just to feel the moonlight on her leaves.

As their voices began to run dry, Bonnie yawned. "Well, I guess that's enough hisssssstory for one day."

"Pardon me?" said Tumbo.

"I said," repeated Bonnie. "That's enough hissss... enough hisssssss..."

It sounded like someone was adding s's each time she tried to say the word—and the s's were coming *closer*. The dark vegetation parted, and both Tumbo and Bonnie drew back in tandem surprise. A large slithering creature had emerged from the grass, and it was hissing straight for them.

CHAPTER SEVEN

✳ GREAT SNAKES ✳

The enormous serpent glided out from the underbrush and curled to a graceful stop right at the base of Bonnie's trunk.

"Did someone say 'ssstory'?" the creature whispered. Its head, the size of a watermelon, rose up and bowed. "I was once part of a ssstory."

Bonnie's leaves trembled, and Tumbo's hairs quivered.

This beast could've swallowed me up back when I was flesh and blood, thought Tumbo. *Not anymore, thank flowers, now that I'm a shadow...*

And besides, it dawned on Tumbo that this snake was made of the same transparent gray matter as himself. *A shadow serpent? But how ever did it leave its post?*

Bonnie must have been thinking the same thing, as Tumbo could sense her fear morphing into curiosity.

"And what story might that be?" Bonnie inquired gently.

"One of the firssst," seethed the shadow snake. "And sadly, one of my lassst."

The snake's voice was gentle, but it carried a primeval power that neither Tumbo nor Bonnie had ever encountered before.

"And did you have a name in this story?" asked Tumbo.

"At firssst they called me Serpent. I was never *given* a familiar name, but over the ages I've come to call myself Dalinda."

Dalinda slipped over the grass on her shadowy scales and peered down at Tumbo.

"I overheard your story, Tumbo. The one about the curly hair and the wishesss. Once, in another time, I too was flesh and blood, just as you were. I remember that feeling... of feeling. Though it's been so long. So ssso long."

Her hissing trailed off at the end, and she raised her head to look out over the horizon.

"When I was banished from the garden and made to crawl on my belly, the only world I could fit into was Shadowland. So I left my skin behind."

"Why ever would someone banish *you*, Dalinda?" asked Bonnie. Her question felt like a joke, but she asked it in earnest. She could sense Dalinda had a good heart underneath that scaly armor.

The snake's eyes shot daggers into the past. "I was banished for the crime of ssspeaking truths and encouraging curiosity."

Tumbo remembered an old saying from his days back in grammar school and took the opportunity to flaunt his education. "You know what they say: *curiosity* killed the cat..."

"Oh enough with that saying." Bitterness flicked from Dalinda's forked tongue. "It is only used by your leaders in order to maintain control. Our ruler Dog is more noble, but even he has his flaws. You do know that Dog will most likely keep you here forever, Tumbo, don't you?"

"Keep me here in Shadowland?" Tumbo thought back to The Center. "Jerry never did say how long I would have to 'stay put.'" The words began to sink in. "Truly, Dalinda... for...*ever*?"

Dalinda nodded her colossal head.

"Dog is in great need of temp hires. He hopes you will stay here long enough until your old life feels like a distant dream. Until you forget about those Drifting Dandys entirely. After all, you can't even move on your own. How did you plan to leave Shadowland?"

"I guess... I hadn't thought about leaving... I didn't know shadows live... forever," he whispered. An uncomfortable tingling feeling flushed through Tumbo's shadow body. *To live forever... and never move on my own... ever... again...*

"Dalinda," said Bonnie, "how is it that *you* can move through Shadowland with such ease? You *are* a shadow, aren't you, if I'm sensing correctly?"

Dalinda's translucent tongue flickered. "I've been here for ages—since the time Dog was elected to rule. I have ssspecial permissions." She looked again to the horizon. "In the past I was somewhat of a 'temp's temp.' Instead of filling in for *shadows* who wanted solo time, I would fill in for *temp* shadows, like you Tumbo, when they needed a moment for themselvesss. Although through the ages, I've grown weary of that. As you would say in the Land of Light, I've gone into retirement. Now I roam the land and do as I please."

Tumbo played her words back in his mind. *Filling in for temp shadows like me when they want solo time... what if... what if I could 'use' some solo time...*

Tumbo's eyes *lit up*.

In the darkness of Shadowland, Dalinda stared down in disbelief. Two singe-marks had appeared on Bonnie's trunk.

"Great shadows below, how did you sssmuggle that ssspark over here?" Dalinda hissed.

Tumbo's mind flashed back to The Center. "Oh flowers, did that happen again? Jerry warned me about that spark, it seems to be quite out of my control unfortunately."

Dalinda gaped in bewilderment. "Has one of your shadows ever done that before, Bonnie?"

Bonnie shook her leaves.

"What is this place becoming?" Dalinda rested her head in the bald spot between Bonnie's branches. "Dog must really be desperate. He is not supposed to take temps with light left inside them. I would have thought he would be more careful after those lightbulbsss."

Tumbo's mind was still rummaging through the words that had slithered out of Dalinda's lips. *Keep you here forever...* He knew he had purpose here working as a shadow, which was better than anything he could hope for back in Terra Floss—but not being able to move on his own ever again? *I've already lost my curls, but to lose movement too?* Tumbo remembered his years of dance training, and the countless hours he had put into getting those wish-granting motions just right. *If I lose my ability to move, I may lose myself... completely... and have to live that way... for... an eternity...* His limbs

felt so heavy, but inside, his nerves could have outrun a thundercloud—even Gerald.

Tumbo blinked back to the present.

"Dalinda, do you still dabble in temp's temp work?"

"Did I ssscare you with my talk about 'forever,' Tumbo?" Dalinda glanced down knowingly. Her eyes were warm underneath their milky darkness. "Would you like me to take your place?"

There is some ancient wisdom about this Dalinda. Tumbo stared up at her, then looked to Bonnie. "It's not that I don't want to be your shadow, Bonnie, it's only... I know this is a job and it gives me purpose but... never to dance again, never to perform again? I don't know what the purpose of existing is, if I lose *every* part of myself... forever."

"Forever *is* a long time." Bonnie reached down a branch to give his hand an understanding pat.

"True indeed," said Dalinda. She stared off into the distance again, as if running through the moments of her own foreverness in Shadowland. "I will help you Tumbo. Shadowland is no place for a being with light left inside of them. Though first I must say, my services can't be given without sssomething in return." She placed her head down in the grass next to Tumbo's. "I would like one of your hairs in exchange."

Tumbo closed his eyes. *I will then have only five left.*

He took a breath. "Tell me your wish and I will grant it when I return to the Land of Light."

He said it quick, like ripping off a bandage—so fast that he couldn't feel the pain of his decision until it was made.

Dalinda leaned in so close that her tickling tongue could almost grab the hair itself.

"I wish to have my own ssstory," she whispered.

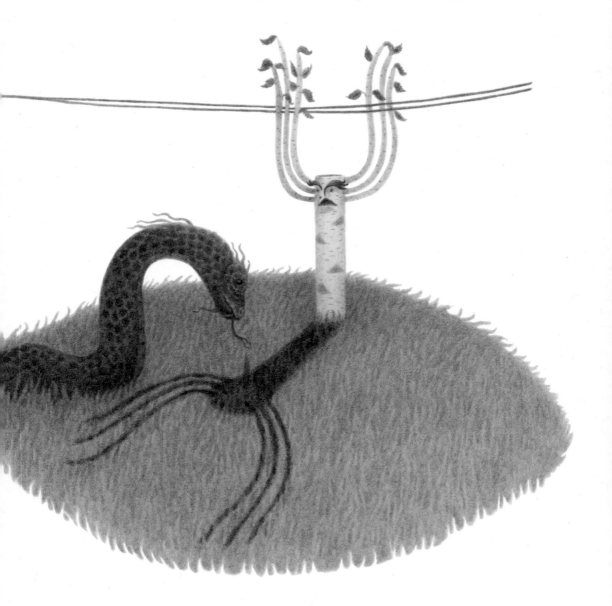

CHAPTER EIGHT

✳ THE FRUIT ✳

The cool night air trickled in through the field. Tumbo swore he could hear it murmuring rumors of his escape plan—a windy warning for the grasses to be on guard, to keep him from escaping at all costs.

Or am I the one spreading rumors so I won't have to go through with my scheme of desertion? Tumbo's

mind reeled. *Who is this new being I am becoming? First eye-rolling, then my sharp tongue—and now—deserter?*

It would be the first time Tumbo had ever broken a rule. He remembered his father sitting him down at the kitchen table as a child, saying: "As an upstanding member of society, Drifting Dandys should never be the sort of beings who break rules." Tumbo knew that staying put was the one and only rule he had been given in Shadowland, and if he broke it...

Where will I go? Will they call me a runaway? Is that who I'll be—an outlaw? Every chiseled feature of Tumbo's finely crafted character had been crumbling away since the loss of his curls.

Dalinda had left soon after their agreement. "There is something special I must obtain in order to free you from your shadow duty, Tumbo. I will return before long to ensure you have enough time to find a hiding spot before Dog catches on. He is not very fond of temp hires roaming the depths of Shadowland."

A hiding spot? thought Tumbo. *Holy Gladiolas! Could I get lost forever in the deep part of Shadowland?* He was in over his head.

"Tumbo, dear, I don't mean to encroach, but you're making me nervous." Bonnie had been feeling his mind churning since Dalinda parted, and she was weary.

"I know, Bonnie."

"Tumbo, what is the worst that can happen? You get lost? You get sent to Shadow Jail?" Bonnie shook her leaves. "*All* Dog will do is place you back here with me. At least... I think that's all he will do. To be honest, I can't remember any shadow temp breaking the rule before..."

Tumbo's heart pounded.

The tall grass behind Bonnie parted and Dalinda re-appeared, returning from her short quest. She dropped something round and gray onto the ground between them.

"Fortune is on your ssside, Tumbo," she said. "The fall fruits are plentiful this time of year."

Tumbo wasn't sure *how* fortunate he was, but he'd come too far now to go back on his word. Dalinda was an understanding serpent, but she was still a serpent.

"Thisss," explained Dalinda, "is a shadow fruit—a shadow apple, to be precise. I'm sure you've noticed that, as a shadow, you haven't had the desire to eat?"

It was true. Tumbo had lost the need for food so completely that he hadn't even realized it had left him.

"You don't need food because, as a shadow, you live from the energy of your Land of Light companion. But out on your own in Shadowland, you'll need to find your own sssustenance. To break the bond with Bonnie, all you need to do is take a few bites of this shadow fruit, and you will have the energy you need to ssstand up."

Dalinda held the apple in her mouth and dipped her head to the ground so that Tumbo could take a bite.

The fruit tasted strange. For the first time in a long time, he was *tasting* again.

The grainy particles swished around in his mouth like television static. It was salty and bitter with a slight tang at the end.

Was this how the apples
in Terra Floss tasted?

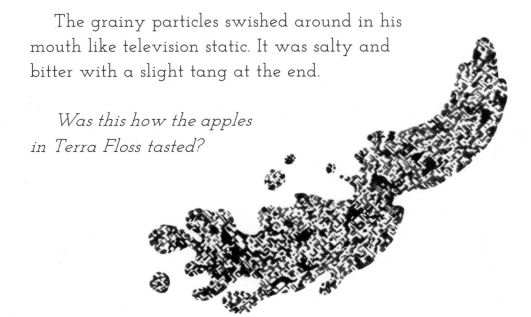

He swallowed and took another bite. Tumbo could feel a drop of shadow juice run down his chin, and he instinctively reached up to clean it away.

He reached up. *All by himself.*

Tumbo looked down at his other hand... and raised it. It felt like he was pulling two pieces of paper apart that had been glued long enough to dry a little. There was a noise, a soft *kirrrrittch* as his arm came loose. Tumbo braced himself on the ground, one hand then the other. He sat up. *Kiiirriiittch*. He stood up. *Kiiiiiirrrriiiiiiiitch!*

He looked at Bonnie. She was so much smaller than he had realized now that they were standing next to one another. No longer could he feel her leaves swishing in the wind or the little ants tickling their way up her trunk. He looked at Dalinda... she, on the other hand, was still very big.

For the first time since the thundercloud and the lightning bolt, Tumbo stood on his own two feet. And even though he didn't know where to go, or what to do, even though he felt like all the heaviness of the worlds was on his shoulders, he *did* know that he could not lie back down.

CHAPTER NINE

✳ BABY STEPS ✳

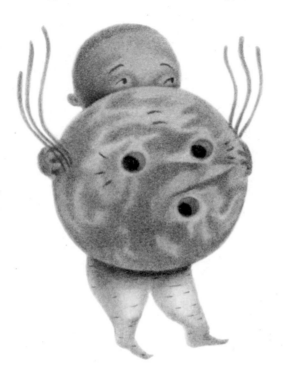

Tumbo stood between Dalinda and Bonnie, his shadow knees wobbling beneath him. Dalinda handed him what was left of the apple.

"Eat the ressst Tumbo, you'll need strength to keep your head up."

And indeed, Tumbo's head felt like a bowling ball in the arms of a newborn.

Had it always weighed this much? How did I manage those lofty twirls in the Drifting Dance Studio with such a head?

He crunched into the apple again, choking down bite after bitter bite until his knees grew stable and he could look out into the distance.

For all the time he had spent in Shadowland, Tumbo hadn't been able to see farther than Bonnie. He had studied her twisting bark, memorized how many leaves clung to each of her branches.

Now Tumbo could see the horizon, that dream of a place into which Dalinda kept staring. There was so much that stood in front of it. Shadow hills and shadow valleys. Craggy shadow boulders and a churning shadow sea. Tumbo could even make out the vague outline of a blocky shadow skyline far off in the distance. Everything was a different hue of darkness, a darkness that felt alive.

"You had better be on your way, Tumbo." Dalinda slid her gigantic head in front of his. "You wouldn't want Dog to find you, he will bring you straight back here to Bonnie. And I do not think he will be amused while doing it."

The thought of the ruler of Shadowland being angry with him made Tumbo's knees even wobblier than before. *Is this unruly plan really worth the risk? Maybe being a shadow is the right path. My work laid out for me without having to lift a finger ever... again. But my entire self... taken away... forever...*

At least if he was lost in Shadowland forever, he would be able to move around on his own like Dalinda.

These shaky legs will have to move whether they like it or not.

"But Dalinda," said Tumbo, "how exactly *do* I find my way out of here? How do I keep from getting lost? Is there a door back to the Land of Light, or some kind of... tunnel?"

"That you will have to find out for yourself." Dalinda wriggled into her new temporary home in the grass. She looked at him with wise understanding. "You will know it when you feel it, Tumbo."

Tumbo closed his eyes and knelt down to give one of Bonnie's roots a squeeze. Teetering to his feet, he put what was left of the shadow apple in his coat pocket and took his first steps towards the horizon.

"And Tumbo," called Dalinda, "when you arrive back in the Land of Light and can grant wishes once again—don't forget about *my* ssstory."

CHAPTER TEN

✳ FEET FIRST ✳

The last time Tumbo remembered walking was in the field outside Terra Floss. He could recall how stable the earth had felt beneath him, how the blades of grass had parted obediently from his footsteps.

The fields of Shadowland were not as compliant. At all. Each time Tumbo placed his shoe to the ground, his foot was thrown back up in the air. Step, throw—step, shove.

It's like having a
disagreement with a trampoline,
Tumbo thought, as he was tossed this way and that.
Over and again Tumbo was thrown entirely off
balance and tumbled down into the grass. He could
have easily stayed there if the ground hadn't given
him such a rough push that he was back up on his feet
again within seconds. Being slammed and shoved was

a tiring way to travel, and Tumbo had to stop soon after he'd started to take the last few bitter bites of the shadow apple. His gray body waved back and forth atop the undulating earth, his eyes combing the rolling landscape for a hiding spot.

Just three hills away, Tumbo spotted a large round boulder perched atop a grassy knoll. There were craggy trees growing out of the rock and around its base.

This stone must have been sitting there for ages.

Back at the Wish-Granting Academy in Terra Floss, Tumbo remembered learning that some of the first of their species made homes inside of giant rocks.

Perhaps there is a place in this rock where I can take cover from Dog, he thought.

Now that he had a destination in mind, Tumbo felt ready to venture further into the turmoil of the shadow field. He quickened his pace. Bounding this way and that, he attempted to harness the chaotic buoyancy of Shadowland's terrain to his advantage. Left—jump, right—jump. He began to develop a rhythm. Left—jump, right—LEAP! He was getting faster.

At this rate, I'll reach the boulder within the hour.

The wind picked up and Tumbo could hear a distant rumbling. Were his eyes deceiving him or was the boulder only two hills away?

Right—LEAP, left—BOUND! Jumping deeper into Shadowland, he felt that every step was bigger than the last. Were his legs getting longer or was this boulder approaching *him*? He was so close now Tumbo could see trees waving atop the boulder, with paws scurrying over the ground below it.

Hang on a petal. Tumbo squinted. *Scurrying? Paws?*

Tumbo stopped mid-leap, trying to remain as rooted as a tree trunk. The boulder was *still* advancing. And the rumbling was growing louder. Not only louder, in fact... but... *was this boulder... speaking?*

"YOOOUUUU DAAARRREEEE TOOO BREEAAK MYYY RUUULLEE?" the boulder roared.

I must be off my stamen, Tumbo thought. *Is this what madness sounds like?*

The rock clambered over the final hill that lay between Tumbo and itself. Tumbo could see that this boulder *did* have an opening to hide in after all—a jagged one, right at the front.

The rumbling continued as the boulder sped closer.

"JUUSSST WHEEERREE DOOO YOUUU THIIINK YOUU AREEE GOINNGGG TUMMMBOOOOOOO!"

Tumbo? Did this boulder say my name?

It was so close that Tumbo didn't need to squint anymore. Those were not trees atop this big rock, but rather... fur. Paws below, fur above, and in the middle—a gaping cave full of big, sharp, teeth. This was no boulder. This *was* Dog himself!

If Tumbo could have lost more color as a shadow, he would have. His heart bounced to the ground, and his body fell backwards in a final desperate plea for the wild vegetation to disguise him. The grass was unsympathetic.

"YOUUUUUU WILLL GO STRAAIIIIGGGHHHTTT BACCKK TO YOOUUUR POSSST!" Dog roared.

Tumbo flipped onto his stomach and grasped at the grass to save him. He buried his face in the mud—but it just punched him in the nose.

There was no hiding now. Dog rumbled to a halt and sniffed at the air. Tumbo's coattails fluttered.

"SUUUCHH AA DISSAPOINNTMENNT," Dog growled. Then he swallowed Tumbo up—feet first.

CHAPTER ELEVEN

* A CAVE WORTH CLEANING *

To say swallowed up is a slight exaggeration. In truth, Tumbo was being held in a pocket of Dog's cheek like a piece of hard candy, scrunched between sharp teeth and moist shadow flesh. Tumbo had never smelled anything so foul.

The walls surrounding him oozed gray goo and stank from millennia of neglected dental hygiene.

Was this Shadow Jail?

The stench permeated every atom of the little mouth dungeon. Tumbo tried holding his breath for a moment's relief, but the putrid smell penetrated his nostrils even when he pinched them closed. Tumbo gagged. He breathed in to calm the reflex. He gagged harder. *Short breaths, Tumbo. Short breaths.*

The squishy pocket was just big enough for him to sit against the wall, knees to chest.

"At least nobody else can fit in here," Tumbo said to himself. "I couldn't endure the embarrassment of someone seeing me in this disgraceful state."

"I CAN SEEE YOU," Dog snarled.

Tumbo caught his breath.

"WEREN'T YOOUU WAAARNED ABOUT THE DAANGERRRSSS OF NOT STAAAYIIINNG PUT, TIIINY TUMBOOO?"

A waterfall of goo cascaded down onto Tumbo as Dog spoke. He coughed. "Well... *cough*... yes." Tumbo choked.

"AND WHO HELPED YOU RUN AWAY, WHO GAVE YOU SHADOW FOOD?"

Tumbo pretended not to hear.

"I DON'T HAVE TIME FOR THIS NONSENSE!" Dog roared. "TELL ME OR I'LL SWALLOW—YOU—DOWN!"

Spit rained over Tumbo's head, pouring into his ears and threatening to enter his tightly sealed lips. He couldn't take it.

"It... was Dalinda," Tumbo whimpered. "She gave me a piece of shadow fruit."

He knew it wasn't right to tell on Dalinda, but he would have *perished* in the belly of Dog. Besides, *Honesty is the best policy*... he recalled from some lesson he had learned back in Terra.... back in Terra... *What was the name of that place again?*

Encompassed by rotten slime, the teeth of his cell allowed barely enough space to wiggle a hair. Tumbo was finding it difficult to remember... anything.

"DALINDA?" bellowed Dog. "HOW PREDICTABLE. AND WHAT PRRRAAY TELL, DID YOU OFFER IN RETURN?"

Tumbo's memories felt as slippery as saliva. *What did I offer?*

One by one
his thoughts
were dripping away
with each passing second.

Who is this Dalinda? Tumbo puzzled. *And where ...*

"Where am I?" he asked aloud.

Dog ignored the question. "SUCH ARROGANCE," he ranted. "I GIVE YOU PURPOSE AND YOU RUN AWAY. YOU BREAK THE ONE AND ONLY RULE." Dog trailed off into a growl.

Torrents of spit slid over Tumbo's shoulders. "Pardon me," Tumbo called into the darkness, his anxiety rising. "But could you please tell me where I am?" He began to shake uncontrollably.

"WHERE YOU *ARE*? IS THIS ONE OF YOUR TRICKS? YOU ARE IN THE MOUTH OF DOG, FOOL! DOG, RULER OF SHADOWLAND!"

A deluge of drool washed over Tumbo, nearly filling the cell. He rose to the surface, gasping for air. *Wherever I am, whoever I am, I won't be able to last much longer in this place.*

Tumbo tried desperately to scratch into the fleshy walls surrounding him, but they just hugged him in tighter.

"ALL I'M TRYING TO DO IS PROVIDE COMFORT FOR MY SUBJECTS," Dog lamented.

Tumbo thrashed as Dog bounded over the hills in frustration. He tried to keep his head above the surface of ooze but was repeatedly thrown under, the slippery sides of the enclosure lending no aid.

"I HAVE NEVER NEEDED HELP FINDING TEMPS. I AM A RULER—I AM DOG!" He trailed off again, grumbling, "WHY DO I KEEP GOING WRROONG OF LATE?"

The cell was almost filled to the top with drool. Tumbo gasped at the sliver of air that remained.

"YOU'RE GOING RIGHT BACK TO BONNIE, AND THIS TIME YOU'LL STAY THERE. UNTIL IIIIII RELEASE YOU."

Tumbo gagged. *Is this it? Is this how I stop getting to be whatever I am?*

He took in a final gasping breath, closed his eyes, and sank under.

Dog blustered on, "WHEN YOOUU WERE AS DIRECTIONLESS AS A TUMBLEWEED IN THE WIND, III WAAS THE ONNEE WHO GAVE YOOOUU PURPOSE..."

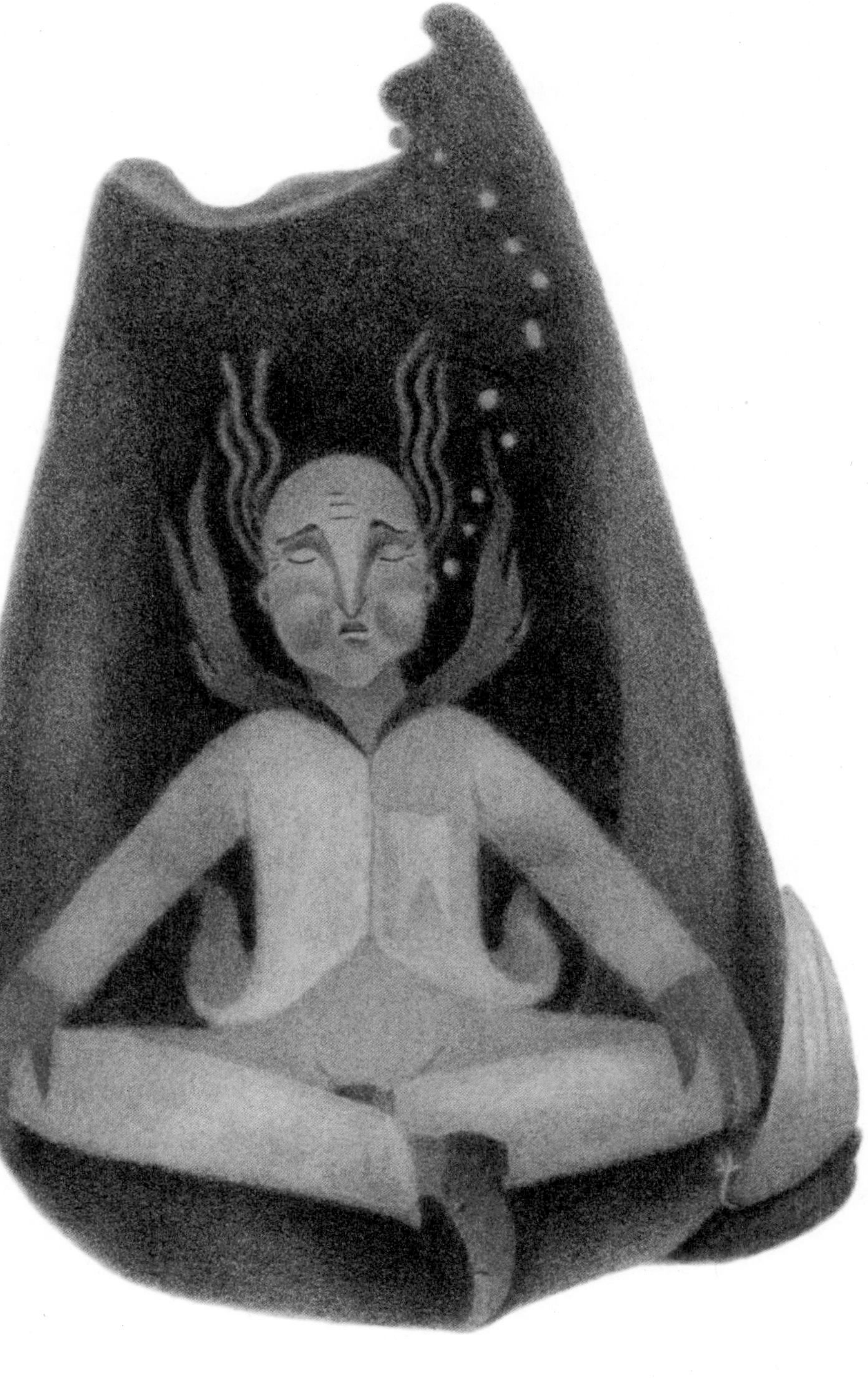

Tumbo's ears perked up from within the slobber tomb. *A tumbleweed... in the wind...* He remembered something about weeds in the wind... Tumbo opened his eyes.

He felt empty, as if the only reality he had ever known was this horrible cave, drowning in goop, a deep voice reverberating through his body. But... *A tumbleweed in the wind.* Those words knocked around in his mind. Tumbo had the itchy feeling he'd *been* someone. But the memory bobbed beyond the surface, just out of reach.

Having sunken to the bottom of the cell, he searched the mushy space with his fingertips. Maybe some clue to his identity had fallen beside him. Nothing... and then... *some*thing. Deep in a fleshy fold Tumbo felt an object. He pulled it to his face. The darkness in the secret pocket was so dense that seeing with his eyes was hopeless—but he could *feel* it.

"WHEN YOU DIDN'T KNOW WHO YOU WERE, I WAS THERE FOR YOU. AND HOW DO YOU THANK ME?"

Tumbo tried not to listen. He could feel the air inside of him running low. *Focus.*

The object was oval-shaped and came to a point at one end. He traced the oval upwards and felt that it continued into a small stem with feathery bits at the end. The feathery bits were damp with saliva, but he *knew* what they would look like dried out: fresh and fluttering in the wind.

An image flew through his empty mind. Tumbo remembered this object, and by name at that. This was a dandelion seed. A Drifting Dandy -lion seed. In the same short time that Tumbo had forgotten every moment of his life, it all came pouring back to him.

"JUST WHOOO DO YOU THINK YOU ARRRE, SEELFISSSHH TUMBO?" Dog sneered.

Who am I? The memory of his first ballet recital flashed before him. The pride of twirling on pointed toe. He burst through the surface of spit, thirsty for air.

"I am a DANCER!" Tumbo's eyes sparked. Two singed spots smoldered on the squishy shadow flesh of Dog's cheek.

"OUCH!" thundered Dog. "WHAT ARE YOU UP TO IN THERE?! DO YOU STILL HAVE... SPARK?!"

Another memory flooded in. He'd had the leading role in the stage performance of *A Dandelion's Wish*. The audience had thrown chrysanthemums at his feet as the curtains closed.

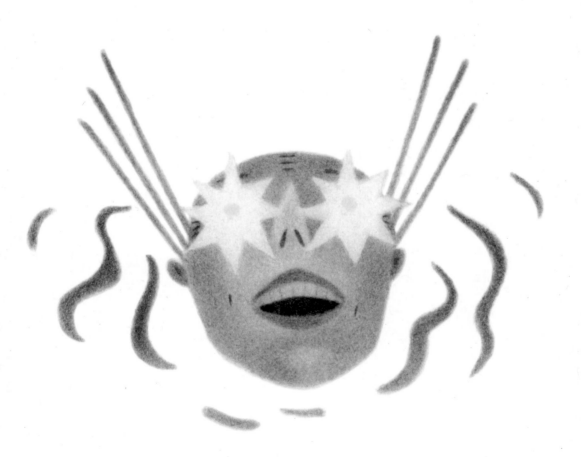

"I am an ACTOR!" Tumbo cried out, his eyes lighting up with exuberance. The singed spots began to burn.

"GREAT SHADOWS BELOW, STOP THAT THIS INSTANT!" Dog howled.

Years of training flickered through Tumbo's mind. "I am a WISH GRANTER!" Tumbo's eyes shot beams of excitement, remembering all that his life had been. (He hadn't gotten to the bit with the lightning bolt yet.)

"YEEEOOOOOOOOOOWWWWWWW," bellowed Dog. Each burst of enthusiasm emanating from Tumbo's eyes stung worse than the one before. It felt like there was a chunk of hot coal tucked into his cheek. "WHAT IS THIS... ARE YOU SOME STRANGE KIND OF... LIGHTBULB?!"

"WISH GRANTER, WISH GRANTER, WISH GRANTER!!" Tumbo shouted, his eyes ablaze. "I am going to be a DRIFTING DANDY!!!"

He had nearly burned through the shadow matter of Dog's muzzle.

"ENOUGHHHH!!!!" Dog wailed, steam leaking from the corners of his lips. "BEGONE, YOU TREACHEROUS

LITTLE TYRANT!! I WILL SEND YOU STRAIGHT
TO THE PLACE WHERE ALL SPARKS WILL TURN
TO SHADOW!"

Dog took a deep breath and spit Tumbo out of his
mouth like a cannonball on fire.

CHAPTER TWELVE

✳ LONG SHOT ✳

Tumbo flew through the misty, gray clouds. Raindrops pelted his cheeks and somersaulted through his six waving hairs. The rain was cold, but clean.

Holy Hydrangea, thank flowers!
He breathed in as deeply as his lungs would allow, then a little more.

Fresh air filled his body, and Tumbo's memory began to return in full, moment by moment. It felt like only yesterday that he had left his childhood home for good. His mother had put her hands on his shoulders in the doorway, fixed his curls and given them a kiss. His father gazed up at his locks with a smile. They both looked at his hair as they said, "You are everything we ever wished for." He had never seen them filled with so much joyful expectation as on that day—the day he left for the Wish-Granting Academy. He felt the weight of responsibility that accompanied his precious locks, but his parents' visible pride filled his life with purpose.

As though awakening from a pleasant dream into harsh reality, Tumbo then remembered the thundercloud and the loss of his curls. His stomach sank. He could nearly feel the tenderness of his scorched scalp again, nearly smell that dreadful stench of the hair that once was, all burnt away: the moment he had realized that everything he ever worked for had disappeared into thin air. Everything his parents had wanted for him. How quickly it was all taken away... from all of them. Tears streamed from his eyes, only to be whisked away by the wind. His anguish left a trail of salty skeletons in the clouds.

Tumbo reached the peak of his trajectory, and his body began its descent toward land. As he plummeted downwards, the clouds around him dissolved, opening windows to the landscape with which he would soon be colliding. It looked much different from the shadowy fields where he had begun his night. The ground below was flat and grassless—it looked hard.

In his former life, a free fall from the clouds would have been cause for panic, but after reliving the loss of his curls, Tumbo felt numb. He fell limply, as if there were an ocean of feathers beneath him. He closed his eyes, but didn't bother to brace himself for the impact.

And what an impact it was.

Tumbo slammed into the surface, but the irritable ground threw him right back up into the air, and the air let him fall, hurtling him back to the surface once again. Up and down and up and down he bounced across the resentful ground, until eventually his bounces became bumps and his bumps became hops. And finally, when the earth had grown bored of fighting, the hops turned into mere vibrations and Tumbo found himself sitting *relatively* still on the pavement. Yes, from what he could tell, pavement.

He stood up. Took a tentative step, tripped—and fell back down.

"Oh for Dog's sake!" Tumbo threw his hands up in exasperation. "Let. Me. OUT OF HERE! Curse that treacherous thundercloud for causing me to come to this terrible place."

There was a distant rumble. Tumbo caught his breath.

"Ouch!"

"Watch it buster!"

"Oohh my filaments!"

"Keep it dim over there!"

What the thistle... Startled, Tumbo turned toward the little cacophony of disgruntled voices behind him. For once it hadn't been the ground itself that had made him fall. *Were those?*... Tumbo leaned down to get a closer look.

CHAPTER THIRTEEN

✳ DARK LIGHTS IN THE DARKNESS ✳

Were those... *lightbulbs?* He must be mistaken, what could lightbulbs be doing in *Shadow*land?

Tumbo squinted, scanning his surroundings. This place was *entirely* different from the shadow fields he had just come from. *Now I must truly be in the depths of Shadowland,* he thought. There was a chain-link fence to the left, a cement wall to the right and in between, a *lot* of lightbulbs. Gathered in different groups, all the bulbs were busy as could be. Some pushed around paint brushes on a dilapidated canvas, while others slid old coins over the pavement using popsicle sticks. The ground had been marked up, turning it into some sort of scoreboard.

A game? His eyes traveled back to the group directly behind him, who had abandoned whatever activity they had been enjoying and were staring at Tumbo. Angrily.

It seems like everyone here in Shadowland has been upset with me lately. Tumbo's heart felt heavy.

"My sincerest apologies for the disturbance," Tumbo said. "I'm new around here." His words came out like a whimper.

"*Watt* did he say?" a tinkering voice called from the back of the group.

"He said, 'He's *neeww hereee!*'" crackled a bulb at the front.

"That fact is glowingly evident." This voice was high and fuzzy, as though played through an old speaker. "You made *quite* the electrifying entrance, young bulb."

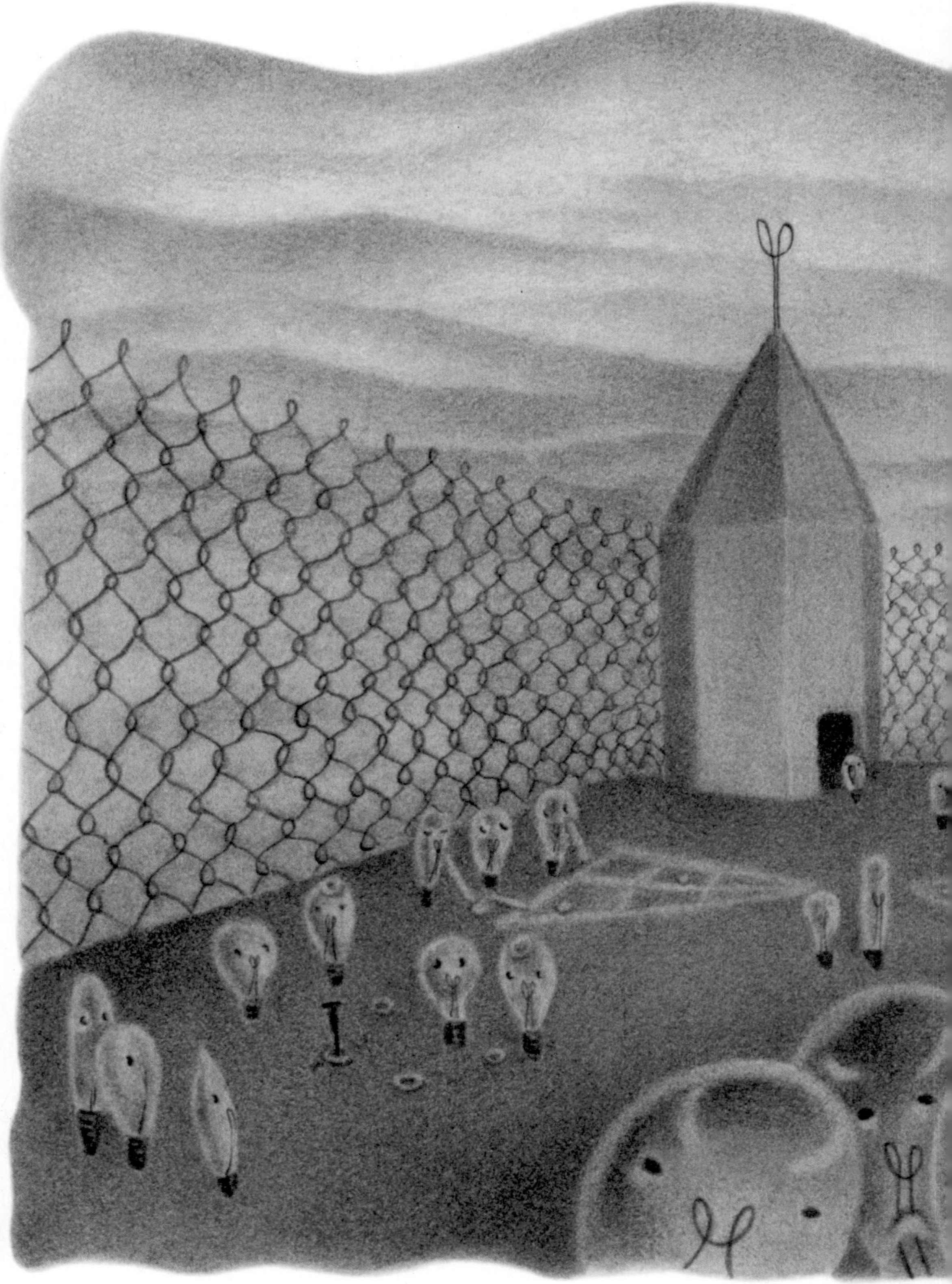

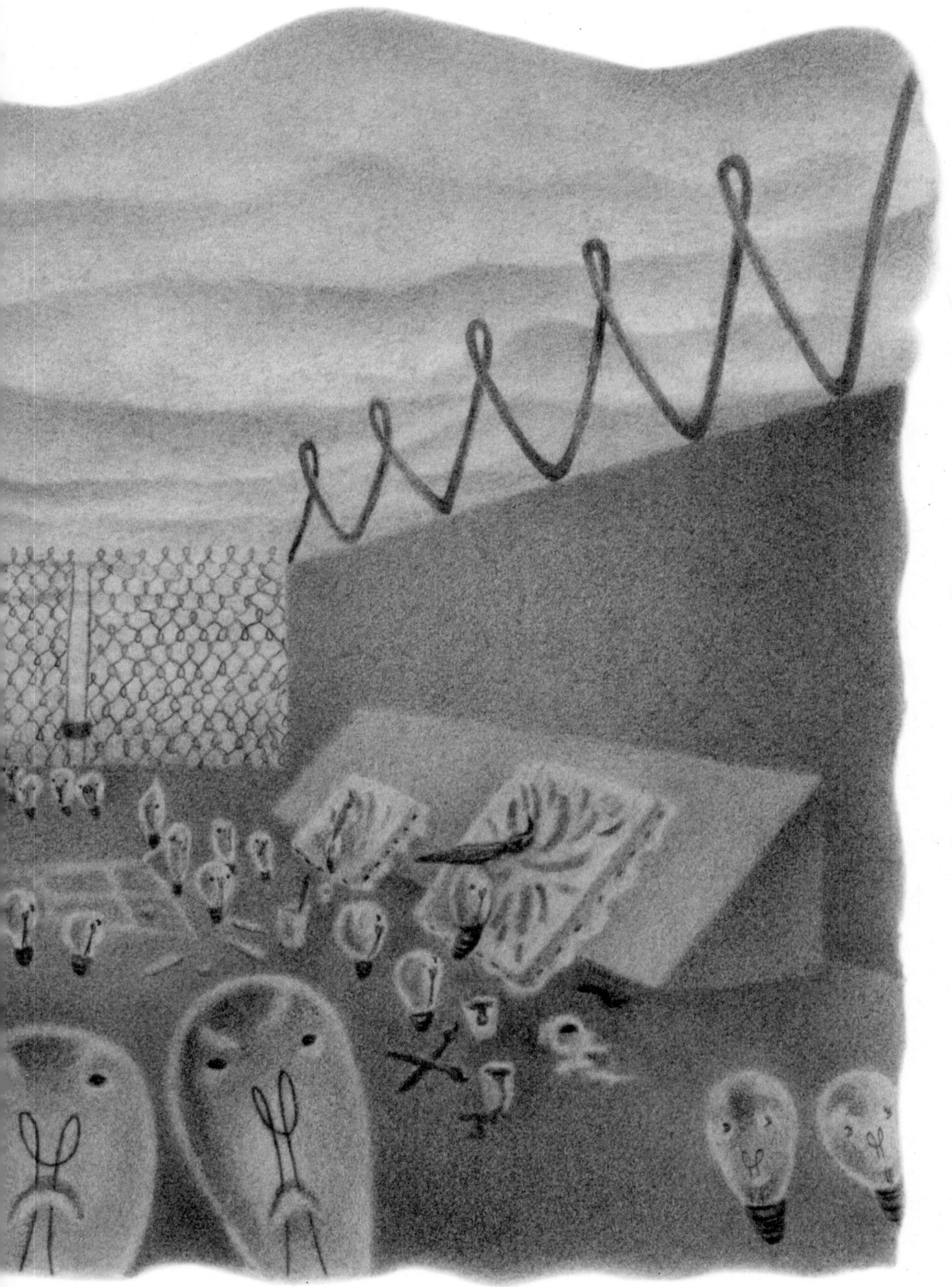

Young what? thought Tumbo. Young, yes, he knew he was in the prime years of his life, but *bulb?*

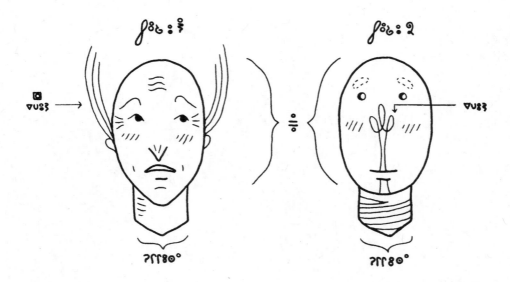

"How manufacturing has changed since my day!" The lightbulb waddled in a circle around Tumbo, looking him up and down. "They've made your cap far too long, and your filaments just stuck recklessly onto the outside of your bulb like that? No care goes into the product anymore—lackluster if you ask me."

The other lightbulbs bobbled in agreement.

Tumbo frowned. *Lackluster? With my big white curls, no one ever called me lackluster...* He put a hand over his round, smooth head and gave a deep sigh.

"Oh Dog, and so fragile too!" crackled the lightbulb.

Tumbo sniffed to himself. "Even if I do find my way back, I am sure all the Flossians will just laugh at me," he murmured through his fingertips. "I'm not even worth a petal. My parents will be utterly disgraced."

The lightbulb realized it may have gone a flicker too far.

"Well, there's no use lecturing a lost cause," the bulb hummed awkwardly. "Might as well get you all screwed-in here at Rolling Currents. Flo! Kelvin! We have a new resident!"

Tumbo wiped a few tears from his eyes and gazed at the ground.

A clinking, clattering noise from a few paces away caught his attention. He could see two lightbulbs tottering quickly through the crowd toward him. They each had a star-shaped sticker glued to top of their bulbs—one had a black star, the other a gray star. The lightbulb with the black star arrived first and stopped at Tumbo's feet.

"Illuminated to make your acquaintance," said the lightbulb. "My name is Flo, and this is my partner, Kelvin." Flo tilted toward the lightbulb with the gray star, who was faltering up from behind.

"Our warmest... welcome," Kelvin panted, "to the Rolling Currents Senior Center for blown-out lightbulbs. Flo and I are the directors here at the RCSC."

They smiled up at him. The lightbulbs were the same translucent gray as everything else in Shadowland, but they had a warmer tone about them.

Maybe not all lightbulbs are so harsh, Tumbo thought. He stared down at them in silence.

"I *said...*" repeated Kelvin, a bit louder this time, "OUR VERY WARMEST WELCOME TO RCSC..."

"Oh," said Tumbo, remembering his manners, "it is a pleasure to make your acquaintance, Flo and Kelvin. My name," he sniffed, "is Tumbo."

"Enlightened to have you here at the Senior Center, Tumbulb," Flo crackled cheerfully. "Would you care for a short circuit around the grounds?"

"Why, it would be my pleasure." Tumbo couldn't resist a little smile and rose to his feet. The pavement didn't throw his legs back as strongly this time, and he almost felt like he was walking normally—just with an extra bounce in his step.

Kelvin and Flo wobbled backwards, guiding him from group to group.

"You'll never get burnt out here at Rolling Currents," crackled Flo. "The long-range of watt we offer will keep you eternally electrified! Shadow meals are served daily at 7am, 12pm and 5pm. And if that doesn't give you enough energy..." Flo nodded to Kelvin.

"Oh, yes," Kelvin sputtered. "If you would kindly direct your lumens over to my left you will see our Electrosize group. If you feel your energy draining, this group meets every morning at 10am for a recharge."

Down on the pavement of the Senior Center Tumbo saw a cluster of lightbulbs with rubber bands stretched across the tops of their bulbs. At the front of the bunch was a bulb leading what seemed to be some sort of workout routine.

"Charrrge to the positive!" The lightbulbs shook toward the sky. "Now—sllllliiiide to the negative!"

The lightbulbs slid to the side and let their bulbs swing to the ground. The instructor continued, "Rooooooolllll around!" They spun slowly on their electrical feet. "Now, let's get lit!"

The bulbs squeezed their facial features together and shook like little earthquakes. "You can do it, my bulbous beauties! Get your lights on!" The instructor yelled, and the shaking intensified.

Tumbo stood as still as an electrical pole. The lightbulbs focused their energy, teetering furiously, until, like lanterns blinking on at dusk, a dim light materialized one by one within each of them.

Tumbo's eyes opened wide like sunflowers. *They too have brought light into Shadowland! And they aren't afraid to use it?*

When the lightbulbs had shaken themselves out, they fell to the pavement clinking and panting, once again gray.

"Great job, everybulby, great job!" The instructor tottered from classmate to classmate, humming with encouragement.

Flo and Kelvin weren't the slightest bit shocked by the spectacle, though they did wiggle with pride. Kelvin turned. "Simply radiating! Wouldn't you agree, Tumbulb?"

Tumbo was shocked. *Whenever my eyes spark it causes destruction. Singeing Bonnie's trunk, nearly burning through Dog's cheek. Creating light doesn't seem like something to be proud of here in Shadowland.*

"At the Job Placement Center I was told not to use my light," Tumbo stammered.

Kelvin looked confused.

"When did you come through The Center, Tumbulb? After the Great Outage, no lightbulb has been allowed into Shadowland."

Tumbo looked away. He didn't want to admit to his new friends that he wasn't actually a lightbulb. *What if they throw me out... or tell Dog about me...* Tumbo worried.

"The... Great Outage?" Tumbo lowered his voice, knowing how naive the question probably sounded.

"You've never heard of the Outage?" Kelvin buzzed. "What a glow stick! Has your fuse been tripped?"

"Kelvin don't be ultraviolet," Flo whirred. "Tumbulb is our guest, show some luminosity."

Kelvin burned warm in the cheeks.

"Don't be put out, Tumbulb," Flo continued. "It happened just a year ago, soon after Dog brought us lightbulbs to Shadowland from the LOL."

"L-O... what?" said Tumbo.

Flo paused in astonishment but tried to appear unfazed.

"LOL... The Land of Light," she clarified.

"Oh yes, of course," Tumbo nodded.

"Maybe you would like a flicker of history to recharge your memory?" said Flo.

Tumbo nodded again, glancing off to the side. Flo looked at Kelvin and then back to Tumbo.

"Well, as you *may* remember," Flo whirred, "the beings who created us back in the Land of Light had the ability to make our power last for a century. But they were extravagant beings. We were given a mere wavelength of energy, so each of us only had enough to light up for a few years at best. Not knowing watt to do with us bulbs once we were burnt out, our creators hid us out of sight, in the *dump*. We sat there for decades, dim and dejected. More and more of us joined each day, tossed away like glitter. We formed burnt-out lightbulb groups to brighten our moods, but it was hard to keep a positive polarity. We felt worthless. No one saw any use for us anymore since we couldn't generate light. They thought we were dull."

The lightbulbs in the Electrosize group had stayed to hear Flo's history lesson. They shook their bulbs, muttering to one another. Tumbo heard one buzz, "Even if we're not watt we used to be, it doesn't mean we're out of power!"

Tumbo bowed his head, remembering all the burnt-out bulbs he and his family had thrown away over the years. *Poor lightbulbs,* Tumbo thought, *just thrown away without a care. There's no more use for me in Terra Floss either. Will the Flossians toss me away too?*

Flo crackled on. "But Dog saw our potential. On one of his circuits to find beings who had lost all purpose in LOL, he was ecstatic when he discovered us. We were the perfect candidates to come work as temp hires in Shadowland."

Just like me, Tumbo thought. The rest of the bulbs from the Senior Center had stopped their activities, tottering closer to hear Flo recounting their tale.

"Observing that there was an ever-glowing number of us burnt-out lightbulbs in LOL, Dog came up with watt he thought was a brilliant idea. He felt drained from centuries of searching the Land of Light for new hires and thought he could set up an automatic lightbulb transfer. The beings in LOL were throwing away burnt-out bulbs daily, and all of us bulbs were miserable in the dump. Dog envisioned an eternity of temp hires without having to lift a paw. He went to the ruler of the Land of Light to form an arrangement. He proposed that as soon as a bulb burned out, it would be energized directly into Shadowland, without Dog having to fetch it. The Ruler of Light agreed in a flash. He had been concerned about our dismal state and was illuminated that Dog could give us purpose."

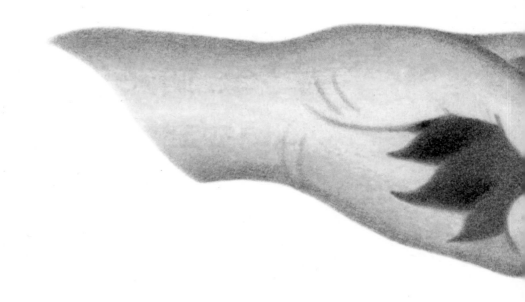

"We all *thought* the idea would be phosphorus..." A bulb from the audience whizzed.

Flo nodded her bulb. "But watt no one knew was that even though we can't light up in LOL, here in Shadowland, we *still* have spark when we're delighted."

Tumbo's eyes widened. *Light up when they feel delighted? Is that why my eyes have been lighting up? From delight? Press my petals, maybe I'm more of a lightbulb than I knew.*

"As the 'light-ups' occurred in higher frequency," Flo crackled, "Dog got embarrassed. He realized this had been a dim idea. Shadows looked at us in fright, scared we would burn a hole through their world at

any flicker. Then came the Great Outage." Flo's voice increased in voltage. "We were pulled from our shadow temp positions and carried here, to this secret socket in the middle of glowhere. We think Dog is hoping that if he leaves us here long enough, our sparks will transform into shadow, and we can be temps once again."

The lightbulbs in the crowd buzzed in a low tone.

"But Shadowland has shown us that we still have energy," Flo beamed. "We lightbulbs will never give up our spark now!"

Never give up their spark... the words filled Tumbo's mind.

"Brilliantly put!" Kelvin buzzed. "We still know how to burn down the house! Don't we, bulbs?"

The buzzing from the crowd reached a higher pitch.

"We built Rolling Currents from the wires up," crackled Flo, "and eventually we'll generate enough energy to go back to the Land of Light. Now that we know we can create power on our own, we can be the conductors of our own lives."

Conduct on their own? Tumbo baffled at the idea. *A good Drifting Dandy goes where they are called... just imagine... conducting...*

The crowd of lightbulbs was galvanized. They hummed, rocking from side to side.

"We will energiiiiizzzee—we will illuminizzzeee, we will conduct our very own liiighht..."

I too want to keep my spark! Tumbo's mind screamed. He looked at the singing bulbs in pure admiration. *I too want to generate enough delight to leave Shadowland! After everything these lightbulbs have been through—thrown in a dump and repurposed, only to be thrown away once again. And yet, they haven't given up; they are still as strong as snapdragons.*

He tapped Flo lightly on the globe.

"Do you mean to say that if I can muster enough delight, I can leave Shadowland?" His voice was hushed, so as not to disturb the song of the lightbulbs.

"If you're in Shadowland, Tumbulb, it means you've had a blow-out," Flo whirred. "Now I'm still not sure *watt* kind of lightbulb you are, but if we have any parts in common, you'll need to generate a *lot* of delight to be able to escape this polarity."

"But where can I find a lot of delight?" said Tumbo.

Flo turned to Kelvin.

"Umbraton," they crackled in unison.

CHAPTER FOURTEEN

✳ SEA IT TO BELIEVE IT ✳

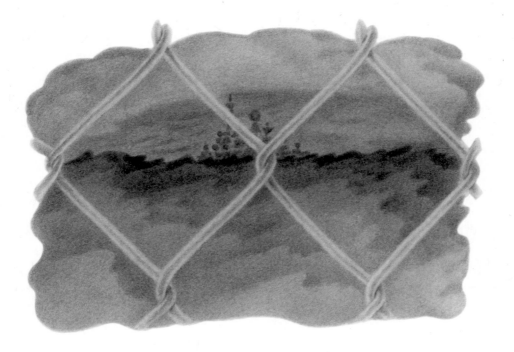

Tumbo stood silent, hoping they would explain just where and what this 'Umbraton' was.

"Phosphorusly?" hummed Kelvin. "This bulb hasn't heard of Umbraton either?"

Flo glowered at Kelvin. "Umbraton is one of the biggest cities in Shadowland, Tumbulb," she crackled. "Maybe it would be illuminating for you to go there."

Tumbo took a deep breath. It was obvious that the bulbs at Rolling Currents Senior Center were becoming suspicious of his silly questions. But he still needed to ask one more.

"And *how* do I get to Umbraton again?"

Kelvin rolled his filaments. Flo waddled through the crowd of lightbulbs who were still singing their ballad. She tilted for Tumbo to follow and led him to the edge of the pavement to a gate in the fence.

"Do you... sea?" she whirred.

Tumbo put his hands on the fence and squinted through the cold diamond-shaped chain links. A salty mist brushed over his knuckles. *Seeds below us!*

Before him was a writhing ocean of darkness. It lapped at the cement edge where the pavement of the Senior Center fell into nothingness. Tumbo squinted through the drizzle. Far across the water he could make out a mountain of tall blocky buildings piled on top of the sea... the island city of Umbraton.

Flo tottered wordlessly over to a shed at the pavement's edge, from which she pulled out two rubber squares and dropped them at his feet.

"I glow you're a sensitive bulb, so I think you may need these to keep you insulated on your journey."

Tumbo picked up the squares. They had gray plastic knobs where one could blow air into them. He blew, and the rubber squares transformed into two tiny flotation devices. *These must have been used to protect the lightbulbs during transit,* he thought.

Tumbo wiggled his hands through the openings, but they were so small that the flotation devices only reached up to his wrists. *Well, a little help is better than none at all...*

He opened the gate. The rusty hinges creaked like an old tree. Tumbo looked back at Flo and the rest of the RCSC bulbs, who had all tottered closer to watch.

"Wouldn't you like to come with me to Umbraton?" said Tumbo.

The crowd shook their bulbs, no.

"Don't you worry about us, Tumbulb," Flo clinked. "We'll stay here at the Senior Center until we've built up a flicker more charge."

Tumbo clenched his teeth and looked across the turbulent sea.

Kelvin and Flo stood at the front of the group, their globes touching.

"Lightspeed, dear Tumbulb. Lightspeed!"

The bulbs rocked from side to side. Tumbo nodded his thanks and stepped through the gate. He braced himself for the icy water, took a deep breath, and fell into the waves—with a *gloop*.

CHAPTER FIFTEEN

✳ CHANGE OF COURSE ✳

Within mere moments, the swift current of the shadow sea had carried Tumbo far away from the lightbulbs and RCSC. He flailed his arms wildly, fighting to stay afloat in an ocean that surely wanted to swallow him up.

"Wicked waterlilies, you will not take me, vicious sea! I will keep my spark, just like Kelvin and Flo!" yelled Tumbo as he writhed in the waves.

But like the shadow ground before it, the sea slopped back up into his face and straight into his open mouth. Tumbo paused. This water was nothing like the water back in Terra Floss. This water was dense and gelatinous. Once he had stopped thrashing, Tumbo saw that though it *appeared* threatening, this sea had a temperament akin to a bubble bath.

The shadow water was slippery and warm. Tumbo noticed that his head floated effortlessly above the dark gray liquid, which was gloppy in texture and slid away from his skin with ease. He loosened up, letting his body rock to the gentle rhythm of sliding down and soaring over the crest of each wave. The water made a soft sloshing sound, and for the first time since his arrival in Shadowland, Tumbo relaxed. He closed his eyes. His head cruised above the water like a sailing ship, the three rippling hairs on either side of it catching the breeze for navigation. The wind whistled around his nose and into his ears. It seemed... the wind was speaking to him...

Look into the water Tumbo, the wind whispered. *Look into the sea...*

Tumbo obeyed the wind and opened his eyes. The gelatinous wall of the next wave was directly before

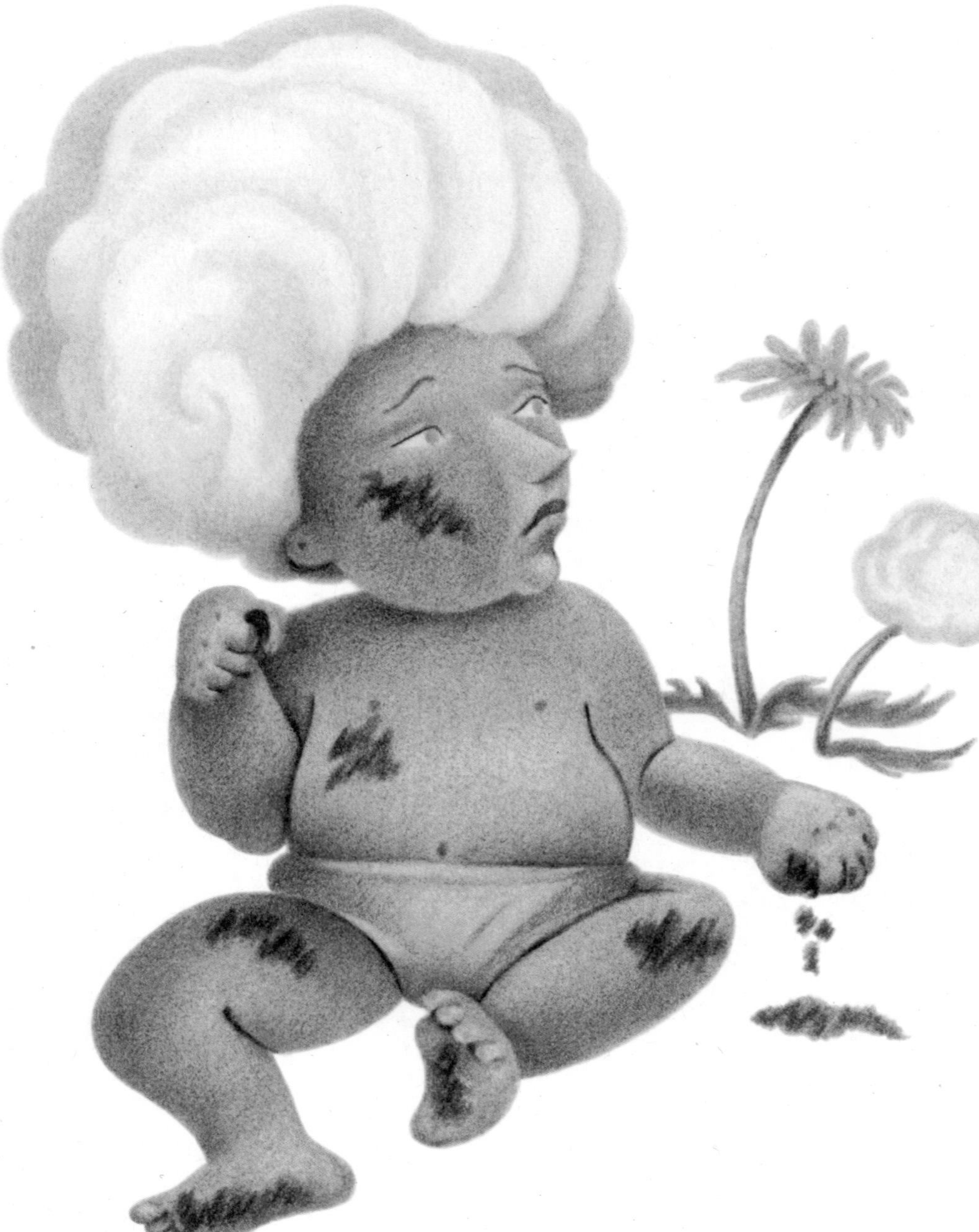

him. But this was no ordinary wave. Floating on the surface of the water was a faint moving picture. Almost like a reflection. *Is that... me?* Tumbo squinted. *Is that me when I was... small?*

There on the wave was an image of a baby sitting in a dandelion patch. It sat smiling in the dirt with a full head of buoyant white curls.

It certainly is me... Tumbo thought, watching as the little boy raked his chubby fingers through the soil. The baby stopped suddenly and looked at someone out of view. His smile turned into a frown, and he let the dirt fall from his grasp.

"Tumbo, put that down. A good Drifting Dandy would *never* have mud under their fingernails." His parents' words appeared in his memory, as if the wind had conjured them up from another time. *I had forgotten how much I enjoyed playing in that mud.* He shook his head, *but it isn't acceptable to have dirty fingernails...*

The wave passed beneath him, and the image of the child went with it. Already, the next memory was approaching. It was him again, but older and standing on the steps of the Wish-Granting Academy, about to enter for the first time. He watched as his hand tentatively turned the brass doorknob. He trembled, twisting it a little at first, then paused and looked around. Tumbo remembered that shameful thought, the cause for his hesitation: *Is this really the only place for me?* The idea had frightened him so completely that he had buried it away as soon as it arose. Tumbo watched his younger self take a deep breath, shake the thought from his fingertips, put on a smile, and walk inside the building.

As Tumbo voyaged on to Umbraton, sailing through this sea of forgotten moments, a fleet of memories trailed in his wake, left behind to break apart on distant shores.

Ahead, Tumbo saw the sky darkening. The air around him grew colder. The wind whistled once again, into his ears. *Don't close your eyes, Tumbo,* it howled. *It is important to see. Even if you think—*

But not even the wind had time to prepare Tumbo for the swell that arose in front of him. From the deepest depths of the ocean floor came a wave so menacing it must have been created in a world of bad dreams. And the moving picture on the surface of that wave? A sky-high image of an enormous... gray... thundercloud.

Tumbo screamed. "I cannot bear it!" His mind was in a scramble. "Please, oh holy honeysuckle, don't make me watch!" Tumbo's legs became as jelly as the water surrounding them.

He tried desperately to swim in the opposite direction, but navigating through the gelatinous water was futile.

Don't look away Tumbo! the wind screeched. *Looking away from this wave is looking away from yourself!*

Tumbo stopped struggling. He turned his head to face the wave, frozen. He watched it rolling towards him, and for the first time he witnessed *it*. There were his glorious curls, bounding through the field. Tumbo reached a hand from out of the water and ran his sorrowful fingers over his now-barren head. He watched the thundercloud, wincing in pain as it shot down its lightning bolt. There was a moment of stillness, and the cloud passed. Tumbo saw his little body struck down in the field, shocked and hairless. It was the very first time he had seen himself since his hair had been taken away. *I look more dreadful than I ever imagined*, he thought in horror.

Tumbo shook with anger at the sight of himself. "It was wrong what happened to me!" he wailed. The wave picked him up, but he beat at the water with a tempest of trauma.

"You wretched thundercloud! I curse you to the vapors of your being!" He grasped at the gloppy water, trying desperately to tear it apart. "YOU TOOK MY LIFE AWAY! LOOK WHAT I'VE BECOME! I'M WORTHLESS! HAIRLESS! All because of YOU!" Tears streamed down Tumbo's face. The wave began to pass underneath him, but Tumbo held fast to its crest. "DON'T YOU JUST FLY AWAY FROM ME AGAIN!" he sobbed, "WHAT DO YOU HAVE TO SAY FOR YOURSELF, CLOUD—WHAT DO YOU HAVE TO SAY!!"

But the wave was only a wave, and though he could hold on for a moment, the current marched relentlessly forward. The memory left him behind without ever speaking a word. Tumbo let out a frustrated whimper and closed his puffy eyes, exhausted. Countless more waves rose and fell beneath him, but no wind could coax him to look at their moving pictures. With a head full of tears, Tumbo floated limply, drifting onward into sleep.

CHAPTER SIXTEEN

✳ THE OTHER SIDE OF DARKNESS ✳

Tumbo's eyes peeled open. Gray gulls soared through the murky sky above him, calling out over the water. He felt the grit of sand beneath his fingertips and the jelly water jiggling over his feet.

Where... what... Tumbo licked his sandy lips. *Have I made it?*

He could hear *other* noises despite the churning surf of the shadow sea—noises that Tumbo recognized from

Terra Floss. Faint beeping horns and humming traffic. *Yes, the city of Umbraton must be close by.*

The air was fresh, and his throat was crusted in salt. Tumbo coughed. Though his mind felt worn through, the bit of sleep he had gotten in the sea had done him well. He removed the flotation devices from his wrists and stood up. The gelatinous water from the shadow sea peeled away from his coattails and dropped to the sand in globules.

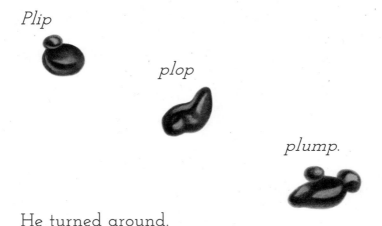

Plip

plop

plump.

He turned around.

From a distance Umbraton seemed to have been built out of toy blocks.

Tumbo tipped his head to the side. "Is *this* what cities looked like back in the LOL?" he wondered aloud.

He trudged across the shadow beach to the road. His legs shook with every step, and Tumbo suddenly realized he hadn't eaten since he'd choked down the apple that Dalinda gave him way back before Dog and Rolling Currents. *If I don't find shadow food soon, I may not be able to keep going*, he worried.

His belly grumbled at him. Tumbo shook his head with determination and stared across the road into the dark streets of Umbraton. His legs quivered. *There must be food in the city.*

He tried to motivate his wobbly knees. "Stand strong, knees!" he bellowed. "We cannot let what that horrible thundercloud did keep us down! We *will* find a way out of here."

Tumbo's knees buckled, and he fell into the sand.

"No!" he shouted. "The hair that gave me purpose was *taken* from me. It wasn't my choice to let it go." A lightbulb flickered through Tumbo's thoughts. "But my ability to *move* wasn't taken away," he whispered. "I have the *choice* to keep moving." Tumbo remembered Dalinda's words... *Dog will most likely keep you here forever.* "If you don't keep going," he said to himself, "you will be *choosing* to lose all of yourself... forever..." Tumbo brought himself back to his feet. Trembling, he moved his body forward.

On the other side of the road, Tumbo could see a metal sign nailed to a post. It was so filthy that he could barely make out what it said. He walked over to it and brushed away the dark grime covering the letters. In large, looping type were the words:

WELCOME TO UMBRATON
GET READY TO EAT, EXPLORE, AND PARTY!

The sign itself had clearly seen its share of parties. Tumbo could hear muffled whooping and yelping coming from inside the city.

So there is shadow food in there after all. He urged his trembling legs to march further.

The outskirts of Umbraton were deserted, but the closer Tumbo got to what he presumed was the city center, the more shadows filled the space around him. This was surely where shadows came to feel solo. *Magnificent marigolds,* thought Tumbo, *are they elastic!* These beings had no definite form, but instead grew larger and smaller with every movement they made. *I hope my static appearance doesn't bring unwanted attention.*

But the shadows were far too preoccupied with their merrymaking to notice him.

The farther Tumbo wandered, the livelier the city grew. He could hear strange twangs and reverberations pulsating out from some of the buildings—shadow music? The doors of these loud buildings were blocked by lines of restless shadows waiting to be let in by puffed-up shadow bouncers. Other establishments had their doors open to anyone who walked past.

Could these be restaurants? Tumbo wondered. He peeked in through one of the doorways. *Indeed!*

At a long counter, shadows sat on tall stools and slurped up dark gooey shakes from transparent goblets. They relished in the food that kept them from needing to lie down. Plates piled high with lumpy treats were slung to various patrons by the elastic arms of the shadow waitstaff. Like expert spiders maintaining a web, the servers were refilling goo cups, cleaning away half-eaten globby leftovers, and giving shadow change—all at once.

Wait, shadow... change? Tumbo focused on one customer who was taking out a wallet to pay. His heart sank at the realization.

Shadow food costs shadow *money*. "I have no way to pay for such refreshments," Tumbo muttered. It wasn't worth searching for a menu; it would be too embarrassing if his pockets were empty when it came time to pay.

Back in Terra Floss he'd often seen people looking in street gutters for dropped coins. Of course, a *respectable* Drifting Dandy would never dream of doing such a thing. *But maybe it doesn't really matter what a Drifting Dandy would do,* he thought.

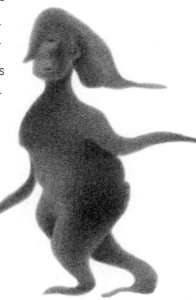

Tumbo walked to the edge of the sidewalk and kneeled down. As could be expected in many solo destinations, the gutter was filled to the brim with shadow trash: bits of transparent paper, matte black disposable cups, a ball of gooey... something... Tumbo scrunched his face together and plunged his hand down into the little garbage mountain.

He was tentative at first, swishing his hand briskly from side to side, hoping to happen upon a piece of currency and not accidentally linger on something foul.

"Good thing my mother isn't here to see me now," he muttered to himself. "If she thought *dirt* under my fingernails was bad... poppies preserve us..."

A group of shadows waiting to get into a dance hall across the street began to mutter and point in his direction.

How utterly humiliating, Tumbo thought. He wished he had some way to cover his face, but alas, there was no hair to hide behind now. The shadows kept glancing over at him, chuckling and whispering.

Tumbo shrunk into himself. He tried to minimize his movements. *If I only dig a little, maybe they will grow bored and forget about me...*

But this hesitant strategy proved unsuccessful. "Oh thorns," he mumbled, "I will never find any money poking around like a pansy. I simply need food or I cannot go on." He sighed. "There has to be *something* in here." Tumbo tried to put aside his fear of what the shadows by the dance hall would think and began desperately scooping and inspecting each pile of waste like a prospector panning for gold. His belly grumbled. And then—

"EUREKA!"

Tumbo pulled an object from the heap and held it high. His eyes *lit up*, slightly burning the edges of his sacred treasure. The shadows waiting at the dance hall shrieked in terror—

"Not another one!" He heard a shadow scream.

"I knew that odd shadow was up to no good!" another shouted.

"Let's get out of here before he burns a hole right though our tendrils!" The shadows bumped around like dewdrops in a saltshaker and quickly dispersed.

Should I run away, too? Tumbo sat frozen on the curbside. *What if they notify the shadow authorities? Are there even shadow authorities?* But Tumbo was too weak to even consider running. He held the object he had found up to his face. In the muck it had felt round and flat—just how he remembered coins feeling back in Terra Floss. But upon inspecting it more closely, he saw that this coin was wrapped in something transparent. This treasure was better than a coin; *this* was a piece of candy.

"And it is a *wrapped* piece of candy," whispered Tumbo.

He twisted the sides of the wrapper apart and plunked the candy into his mouth. Like the shadow apple, it tasted salty and bitter and had a slippery texture. He tucked it into the corner of his cheek, letting its melty runoff drip down his throat without having to taste much. *It's not an apple, but it's something.* Already he could feel his knees calming.

Now that the judgmental crowd from the dance hall had fled, Tumbo could hear the other noises of the city. He sat on the curb sucking on his candy and closed his eyes. Shadow cars passed by with a whirr, a muffled chattering emanated from the restaurant next door, and sirens droned down a distant street.

I wonder what kind of emergencies happen in Shadowland... he thought. His ears pricked up as the siren wailed on. *It has such a heartbreaking tone. In Terra Floss sirens are automated... but here, the cry wavers and changes as if it's coming from someone really in pain... fascinating.*

"wwwwAAAAAaaahhhhyyyyyyoooOOOooHhh wwwhhHHhhyyyyyyyyyyDDoooeeesssnnNnooooO OOOooooooboddyyywwwaaaAAannnttttmmMMee eeeeeeeeeeEEEEeeeeee," the siren moaned.

"Gosh, call me daisy," muttered Tumbo, "but I swear I can even hear words in that alarm bell. They must really be sensitive souls, these Umbratons, to have such a heartfelt siren."

The wailing grew louder.

"iiiiiIIIiiiiieeeeWWiiiiiiillllllnnNeevvvvverrrrrrrrrrr bbbbBEEEEEeeeeeLLLlllOOOOOooooovveeddd."

"Never be loved?" Tumbo opened his eyes and scratched his bald head. "Well, that's an odd thing for an emergency bell to say..."

"woOOOoooorrthhlessssSSSsss," it rang out, "ccOOo ooommmppplleeeEEEeetteelllyyywooOOorrtthhlessss."

Tumbo leaned his head closer to the trash in the gutter. That was no siren. The howling was coming from inside the garbage pile. He knew he should probably move on—one of those dance hall shadows had most certainly alerted the authorities by now... but the whining sounded so desperate—a bit pathetic, yes, but he could almost smell the despair.

He didn't care what the shadows would think of him anymore. Tumbo reached his hand back into the smelly gutter, brushing away slimy popsicle sticks, bottle caps, and half-smoked cigarettes with sticky gray lipstick smeared on their filters. The cry grew louder. Tumbo spread the garbage away as if his hands were parting a polluted sea. A bent straw pushed to the left, a crushed can of goo to the right. The wailing intensified. He had nearly reached through to the pavement when—there at the top of a mound of dark black muck, Tumbo could

see something small, round, and smooth poking out.
He pinched two fingers into the sludge and plucked
out the culprit. The crying ceased.

CHAPTER SEVENTEEN

✳ BROKEN HEART OF STONE ✳

Tumbo held the piece of trash in the palm of his hand, and, using one of his coattails, wiped the remaining black slime from its face. From *all* of its faces, that is. As he tenderly cleaned the object, he could see just what all this digging had won him. *This* was no piece of garbage—*this* was a diamond ring! And not any old diamond ring: this diamond was as big as a tulip, worlds larger than any diamond Tumbo could have ever dreamed into existence.

This ring could buy an eternity of shadow food, he thought. He let his stained coattail fall to the side without a second glance.

"Are *you* the tiny trinket who was making such a ruckus?" said Tumbo.

He was only trying to make a joke, but the ring broke into hysterical sobs. It sniffled pitifully up at Tumbo.

"A trinket?! Is that what I've become? A mere trinket?! First, I am flushed down the toilet and now I'm being teased by a derelict!? *I* am the Earl of Diamond, for Dog's sake!"

"Wait—you mean to tell me you've been in a toilet?" Tumbo dumped the ring back into the muck with a plop. He suddenly recalled where things in the gutter *came* from. *Malevolent mushrooms, the candy! The candy that I ... that I ...* Tumbo swallowed hard, trying not to think about it.

"Dumped again?! I just can't take all this rejection!!" The ring screeched from below. "OH WOE IS ME!"

Tumbo looked down at the poor creature, at the way it lay there in the gutter flat on its back—helpless.

This looks… familiar… thought Tumbo, remembering how the shadow sea had shown him his own likeness after the lightning bolt. "Alright, alright…" Tumbo retrieved the ring, glancing from side to side. "You sure can throw quite a big tantrum for such a little ring."

"Like I told you, I am an Earl, not just some little old ring."

Tumbo sighed. He tried to put aside thoughts of the putrid pipelines through which Earl had traveled not so long ago, along with his worry that if there *were* shadow police, they were *definitely* on their way by now.

"Okay, Earl. Where were you before you ended up in the gutter? Perhaps I can take you back to where you belong?" Tumbo had nowhere else to go anyhow.

"Take me back?" Earl sniffed. "She'll never take *me* back."

"Who's *she*?" asked Tumbo.

"One of the most eloquent maidens in all of Terra Floss! Her betrothed had me cut from the finest gemstone; my carats are in the thousands, my value beyond measure—I'm sure you have never seen a diamond so magnificent as I! But *nobody* seemed to care two facets about any of that—after her fiancé broke off their engagement, I was flushed away without a care."

"Wait a wallflower, you're from Terra Floss!?" Tumbo couldn't believe it. "Blustering blossoms, dear Earl, I, too, am from Terra Floss! Were you also brought here from the Land of Light?"

"Yes, yes," Earl said indifferently, continuing his rant, "and now... my life is meaningless, purposeless! Even if I were to find another finger to embrace, well... turn me over...do you see... do you see it?"

Tumbo flipped Earl over in his hand. There was a tiny chip missing from one of his well-cut corners.

"Ah, I see," Tumbo nodded. "But the chip is quite small, Earl. It doesn't look like anything to get clouded-up about."

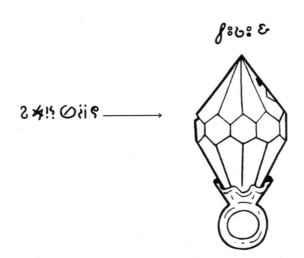

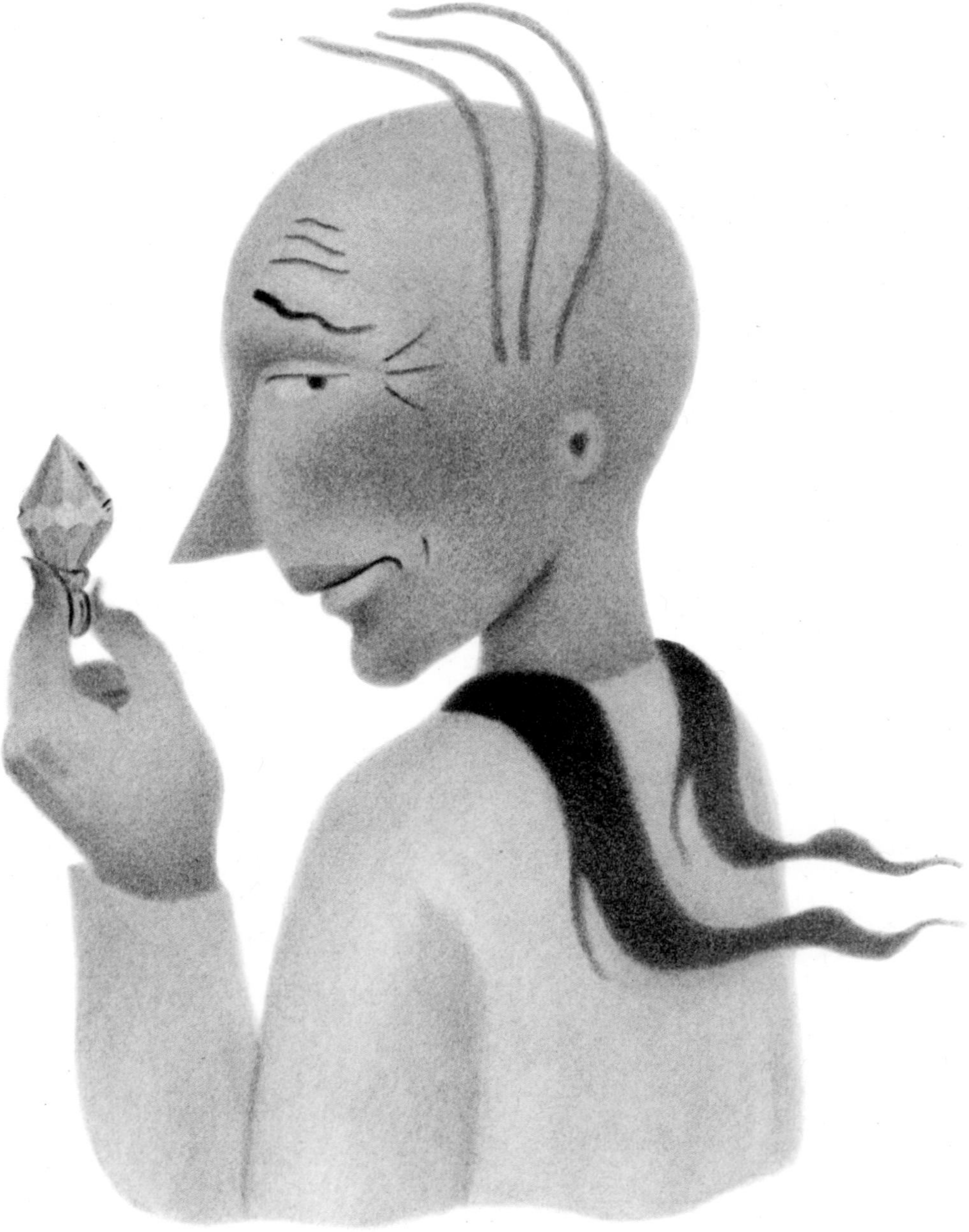

"Are you saying this chip... is not... a big... DEAL? I have a flaw, you fool! A blemish, an *im*perfection! My life is over! Who would ever want to wear such a monstrosity?" Earl resumed his wailing.

Tumbo sighed. As much as he didn't want to admit it, he could see a lot of himself in this little fellow. *Was I really this pathetic?* thought Tumbo. *Or rather—am I really this pathetic?* He couldn't help but let out an embarrassed chuckle.

Earl's crying grew louder. So loud that if it wasn't for the sound a megaphone blaring, STOP IN THE NAME OF THE SHADOWLAND POLICE FORCE, YOU ARE UNDER ARREST, Tumbo may not have heard the *actual* sirens or noticed the *actual* shadow police car that was speeding right toward them. His heart skipped a beat. Someone from the crowd *had* called the authorities after all. Tumbo didn't think. He threw Earl into his coat-jacket pocket and made a run for it.

CHAPTER EIGHTEEN

✳ HILMA ✳

Tumbo dashed down the street at top speed. *I am beginning to see the many other uses for my years of dance training*, he thought, leaping across the pavement like a fugitive ballerina. But not even the most exquisite ballerinas can outleap an automobile, even with perfectly executed *jetés*. The shadow patrol car was quickly catching up to him.

"STOP IN THE NAME OF THE SPF," boomed the megaphone. "FAILURE TO COMPLY IS PUNISHABLE BY DOG!"

Earl jostled around in his coat pocket. "What is going on out there? Where are you taking me?!"

Tumbo didn't answer, he was too busy staring down the road ahead. Darkness. The street was coming to a dead end. He glanced back—the police car was only a few leaps behind him.

I'm done, he thought. *Here lies Tumbo, convicted felon in Shadowland.*

He looked to either side. There was nowhere to turn, no pile of something or other to jump into—all he could see was what lay straight in front of him: a black metal guard rail, and beyond that... nothingness. *Am I back at the ocean already?*

The wind hissed through his six bouncing curls, as each long stride brought him closer to the guard rail. The shadow police car nipped at his heels, while the buildings on either side of him stood as cold and silent as tombstones. His only chance was the nothingness ahead—which was fast approaching in three steps, two steps... one. Tumbo clenched his fists, closed his eyes and leapt at the railing.

"Oohh, no you don't!" A bold voice echoed down from above.

A shadow arm extended swiftly from a nearby building. It grabbed onto the back of Tumbo's collar mid-leap, abruptly pulling him up and away from the patrol car. One moment he was flying forward into the abyss, and the next he was ascending backward into the sky. Tumbo choked back a breath.

"They've got me!" he gasped in abject horror. "This is how it must feel to be a fish pulled from the sea."

And just like a fish plopping onto the deck of a sailing ship, Tumbo was pulled into a shadow building and flung onto the floor of an apartment. He sat up in alarm and wriggled, panic-stricken, into the corner of the room.

"*Now* will you tell me where you are taking me?" Earl grouched at him from inside his jacket pocket. He removed Earl shamefully.

"I don't know," Tumbo whispered. "But hopefully somewhere better than the gutter."

Earl was silent. Tumbo slipped him back into his pocket.

"What a special ring you have there." The voice that had echoed down from up high now came from across the room.

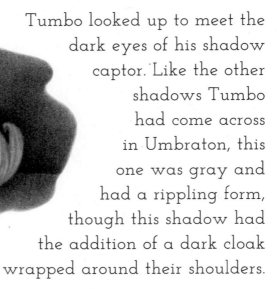

Tumbo looked up to meet the dark eyes of his shadow captor. Like the other shadows Tumbo had come across in Umbraton, this one was gray and had a rippling form, though this shadow had the addition of a dark cloak wrapped around their shoulders.

"My name is Hilma," said the shadow. "I was at my window when you shrieked down below and I saw that spark you made with your eyes. You have to be careful with tricks like that around here."

Tumbo bit his lip and nodded in agreement. "My name is Tumbo. Are... you a member of the Shadow Police Force?"

Hilma laughed. "*Me*, shadow police? Ha! I *saved* you from the SPF, silly!"

Tumbo was taken aback. "But why aren't you afraid of me like all the other shadows?"

"Not all of us are such lightweights." Hilma sat down on the floor next to Tumbo. "Most of the shadows in Umbraton are just here for the solo season, but I live here. I've only been able to read about the temp shadows who ignite in the papers; I've never gotten to see one for myself. Maybe that's why my curiosity outweighed my fear. That spark of yours—I find it intriguing."

"That spark?" Tumbo glanced to the side. *She seems like a trustworthy shadow,* he thought. "I have that spark because... I think I brought it from the Land of Light... that's where I'm from." Tumbo looked down. "I guess there's no use keeping it a secret... as you may have already presumed, I was a shadow temp-hire. But..." Tumbo paused, "I ran away from my duties once I found out that Dog might try to keep me in Shadowland forever."

Hilma raised her brow.

Tumbo scrambled to explain his desertion. "My whole life I have loved the freedom that movement brings me—dancing, performing, wish granting. The curly white hair that gave me purpose was taken from me... but movement wasn't. I have chosen to keep moving, and to find my way back to the Land of Light."

Hilma tilted her head to the side, taking in the sudden flood of information.

Tumbo continued to ramble through his thoughts, talking more to himself than to Hilma. His hands quaked. "The lightbulbs said I need a lot of delight to find my way out of Shadowland, but I still wonder, is it even worth trying to go back to the LOL? Will the Flossians ever be able to accept me the way I am now?" He began to doubt himself once again. "Dandelions preserve us, maybe Dog's right, maybe being a shadow *is* my new purpose."

Hilma sighed and patted his knee. She got up and went into another room. Tumbo heard dishes rattling and liquid pouring. She returned with a dark plate of something, and a dark glass of something else.

"Tumbo, you seem jumbled—and hungry. I think before you decide what your purpose is, you should have a bite to eat."

CHAPTER NINETEEN

* ALL FILLED UP *

It was a good thing Tumbo had his eyes fixed on the shadow food, because as soon as he saw it, they lit up. Two burn marks seared the rim of the dinner plate.

"Well, I can't say I blame them for being frightened of you," Hilma chuckled.

Tumbo took the plate—he was hungrier than he'd realized. He barely glanced at the different inky blobs piled on the platter before greedily pushing them into his mouth. The shadow food popped and fizzled on his lips; kinetic particles lodged in his teeth and swished around his tongue. It had the same horrible taste as the apple and the candy—but it was starting to grow on him. He slurped down the glass of thick black goop, lapped up the last drizzles from his hands, and licked the plate clean. Tumbo was finally full.

The frenzy of hunger no longer clouding his vision, Tumbo could focus on the space around him. The furniture in Hilma's home was sparse. To his right, a velvet sofa stood before a short stone table. There was only one picture hanging on the walls of the room: a large photograph of the shadow seashore. Tumbo quivered and continued scanning the space. A worn, braided rug lay off in the corner underneath a wooden easel. Pallets and paint-filled cups were scattered around the easel's base, while stacks of painted canvases stood politely out of the way against the wall. Tumbo's eyes wandered back around the room to Hilma. "Hilma!" Tumbo said. "I nearly forgot to thank you for saving me." He dipped his head in gratitude. "Come to think of it, what in the bluebell inspired you to save me after all?"

Hilma laughed, "Oh, I've made a hobby—or rather—a *living* of meeting different sorts of shadows. I work as a portrait painter here in Umbraton. I could tell from that spark you must be a *truly* different sort of shadow. Besides, I like fooling with the SPF when I can get away with it." She winked. "So, my dear Tumbo, do you want to have a look at my portraits?" Hilma cleared Tumbo's *very* empty plate and brought it back to the kitchen.

"Why, sure," he said.

"Can I see as well?" A muffled voice came from inside Tumbo's jacket pocket. In his wave of hunger, he had completely forgotten about—Earl! Tumbo pulled him out and held him between his thumb and forefinger.

Hilma smiled. "*You* can have a front row seat." She led the two of them over to the corner that served as her studio. She flipped through the stack of canvases.

"Here's one I did of a young shadow who was visiting Umbraton for the first time... and this one is of our neighborhood librarian. A local treasure."

"Wow," Earl cooed. "You really have a talent for capturing shadows!"

Hilma's cheeks grew darker, and she swished her cloak.

Each painting had a black background, and in the center was a blobby gray form. *I feel like I could paint that with my eyes closed,* Tumbo thought.

"They're... very interesting," he said.

Hilma laughed. "It's all in the details," she said, "and in the feeling. I would love to do a quick portrait of you two, if that would be all right? Portraits help me remember all the shadows I meet here in Umbraton."

"But of course!" said Earl, nearly jumping from Tumbo's fingertips.

"I thought portraits were painted of those who've accomplished something in life," said Tumbo. "I'm a nobody."

Hilma smiled. "Everybody is somebody. Now if you could sit here on this stool, Tumbo, and place your friend—"

"Earl of Diamond, pleasure to make your acquaintance," Earl eagerly interrupted.

Hilma made a small bow in front of him. "I beg your pardon—Earl, was it? If you could just place *Earl* on your finger, Tumbo, we'll be all set."

Tumbo looked down at Earl. "I know I'm no one special, but can I have the honor of being your wear-er?"

"A finger's a finger," said Earl. His words were casual, but Tumbo sensed his enthusiasm to be worn again. Fortune was on their side, and Earl fit perfectly on Tumbo's left pointer finger. He wiggled into place, making sure his chip was facing behind him, and gave his best smile.

"Earl, you look great," said Hilma. "Now Tumbo, please hold your chin up a bit higher, and both of you stay as still as possible."

Tumbo straitened up. "Thank you," said Hilma. "This shouldn't take long." Hilma placed her easel between them and grabbed a paintbrush. She dipped it into a cup of black goop and began.

"So Tumbo," said Hilma, "tell me something about this nobody that you are."

"Well... I was supposed to be somebody, but then all my curls were taken away, and now I can't be the somebody I thought I was going to be." Tumbo's shoulders drooped.

"Sit straight, please," said Hilma, smiling. Her paintbrush made small scratching noises as it traveled around the canvas. Tumbo sat up.

"At first, I was honored that Dog picked me as a temp hire," he continued, "but to lose all of myself, forever... Then again, who is *myself*? Ever since I came here to Shadowland, I don't know who I am anymore. I've been a rule-breaker, a fugitive. I'm not who I prepared myself to be, that's for sure."

Hilma scratched away at the painting. "We are all full of surprises," she said, dipping her brush. "If I may ask, who *were* you prepared to be back in the Land of Light?"

Who... was I? he thought. Memories from the life he once led fell like a veil before Tumbo's eyes. *Joyful memories that now taste so bitter, now that they have all been for nothing.* He felt like he was back in that sloshing sea, but this time when the memories came there wasn't a wave to wash them away. The only way to let them go was to let them out, through his mouth.

Tumbo's lips creaked open. "Back in Terra Floss," he recounted, "my father used to tend to my white curls as diligently as he did his dandelion patch —no hair was ever left out of place. I loved the way it felt when he combed through them with such care." Tumbo patted the ghost of his locks. "My parents spent countless hours helping me through wish-granting drills each night so that I would be in top shape to get into the academy. I adored their attention. They trained me so well, when I got to school all my teachers marveled at my abilities. My dance professor told me I was a true talent. When the headmaster shook my hand at graduation he said, 'Tumbo, you will make great wishes come true in your lifetime. You may be the best wish granter this land has ever known.' But," Tumbo continued, "my precious hair was blitzed away forever, and now I can't be who they all thought I was going to be. They worked so hard to help me succeed, had such high hopes—I can't even imagine how disappointed they'll be to see me now."

Moment after moment poured out until Tumbo felt as though he were sitting in a bowl of memory soup.

But unlike his favorite rosehip soup back in Terra Floss, lurking at the bottom of this broth were overcooked chunks of loss and shame. Luckily, Hilma was there with a ladle to scoop him out.

"Have you enjoyed your life so far?" she interrupted.

"Well... yes. Yes, my life was positively delightful... all the praise and anticipation. I was really going to *be* someone."

Hilma put down her brush and stuck her head out from behind the canvas. "And you're *not* someone now?" She was no longer smiling.

"I mean," said Tumbo, "I'm no Drifting Dandy."

"You know, Tumbo, my parents also had an idea of who they wanted me to be. They hoped I would stay linked to my light companion up by the border where Shadowland connects with the Land of Light. Like what you did in the beginning of your time here. But that kind of life was never for me. I had a chance to make my own way and stay in the city. I wanted to be my *own* shadow. They may have been disappointed, but I love my life, and I love what I do."

Hilma leaned back behind her canvas and continued painting.

She's a conductor, Tumbo thought. "But my parents will simply *wilt* if they see what happened to me," he said. "My curls were all they ever talked about."

"Well, now they can talk about something else." Hilma glanced up and winked. "I know that right now you feel you've lost your only purpose, Tumbo. It sounds like you've been through a lot, and you had a lot to live up to. But perhaps the purpose of your journey isn't about who you will be, maybe it's about who you *are.*"

"But Hilma, I don't know who I am," said Tumbo.

"I don't think you've had much of a chance *to* know. Knowing yourself takes time. Maybe now's your chance." She glanced up at Tumbo and Earl to see if there were any details she had overlooked. "I am excited for you. Getting to know yourself is an everlasting adventure." Hilma picked up a smaller brush and added a few final dabs to the portrait. "We are always growing and changing."

She nodded her head at the canvas. "Right, I think that's that!" Hilma turned the painting around and stood up with a smile.

Earl, who had not moved a single facet throughout the entire portrait, erupted with enthusiasm.

"You, my dear Hilma, are a true talent! Look how beautifully you immortalized my sharp angles and charming mystique. Bravo, my dear, bra-vo."

When Tumbo looked at the portrait he saw two unimpressive gray blobs on a black background, one blob much bigger than the other. He walked closer to the painting, trying to understand why Earl was so impressed. He stared, hard. In the same way his eyes had adjusted to the darkness when he first arrived in Shadowland, the longer he looked, the more he could see. Hilma had painted the wrinkles around his sunken eyes and the irregular shape of his leaf-like collar. But best of all, she had captured his six waving hairs swirling around the top of his head... *beautifully*... like a delicate crown.

Tumbo gazed at the way Hilma had painted his hair. It was sensitive and noble. He tilted his head and smiled. The longer he stared at the painting, the more he realized that he actually quite liked the way he looked.

CHAPTER TWENTY

✳ CRUSHING ✳

"I have to leave soon," Hilma said, placing her brushes into a dark wooden box. She collapsed her easel and packed a blank canvas, brush-box, and cup of paint into a large, stained bag.

Tumbo couldn't take his eyes from the painting, at the *way* Hilma had painted him. *I never imagined anyone would be able to see beauty in me after my hair was blown away*, Tumbo thought, *but she has*.

Hilma continued, "Dr. Strata, a well-known therapist here in Umbraton, has commissioned a portrait from me. Would you boys like to come along? I would love the company."

Earl and Tumbo exchanged a puzzled glance. "Come along? To a job?" Tumbo asked.

"Her office is near the top of the tallest building in the city," Hilma explained, "and they have a glass elevator that goes all the way up!" She paused. "Tumbo, you said you need to feel delight to find your way out of Shadowland. Well, I can't think of anything more *delightful*." Hilma gave him a wink.

Tumbo's heart fluttered in a way it had never fluttered before. His cheeks darkened. He began to nod yes, but then remembered what had happened the last time he had been out on the streets of Umbraton.

"What if the police are still searching for me outside? Won't I be recognized?"

"Don't you worry about that," said Hilma. "I have

plenty of extra cloaks in my closet. If anyone asks, I'll tell them you're my apprentice."

"You mean we get to go up in the *Tower Obscura*?" Earl couldn't believe it. "Hilma, you're spoiling us! During my days in the gutter, I always overheard shadows talking about the Tower. It's supposed to have the best view in all of Shadowland! Tumbo, what say you?"

Tumbo looked at their expectant faces. "I say... it sounds delightful."

Tumbo made quite a convincing shadow with the cloak draped around his shoulders and its hood pulled up over his head. No one could have ever suspected there was a fugitive with spark hidden underneath.

Hilma closed the door to the apartment behind them with a clack. "All set? Anyone forgetting anything?"

"I don't have anything to forget," Tumbo said with a slight smile.

Earl nodded. "Earl of Diamond, ready to depart."

Hilma escorted them down the marble stairs that led to the street. The sound of their footsteps echoed between the walls. Tumbo breathed in deeply to calm his nerves. The stairwell smelled musty and cool, as if some of the sea had gotten trapped inside the stone. *What was this feeling he felt every time Hilma looked at him?*

Hilma pushed open the front door of the building. "The Tower Obscura is only a short walk away."

Earl wriggled with excitement. It was his first time being worn in public since the broken engagement.

Maybe I'm not his top choice of wearers, Tumbo thought, *but it doesn't seem to matter a grain of pollen who I am.*

"Earl, are you comfortable?" Tumbo asked.

"Indubitably," Earl replied with a grin.

Hilma handed Tumbo her easel to carry so there would be no doubt that he was her apprentice. At the brief touch of her shadow hand, Tumbo's face almost began to glow.

As they walked, the neighborhood slowly gave way to the hustle and bustle of a big city. The relatively quiet streets around Hilma's apartment grew wider and teemed with shadows going this way and that.

There were little shop windows full of shapeless stuffed toys and figurines. There were eateries packed with shadows giggling to one another as they slurped down frothy gray sodas. A series of large banners draped over buildings advertised a new exhibition at the Shadowland Historical Archive called "Lightbulbs: Where did they go, and will they return?". Tumbo tried to take it all in, but the magnificence of the shadow who strode before him kept stealing his attention. He gazed at the majestic way that Hilma's cloak moved through the crowd. *Like the way her brushstrokes had found beauty in my scarred complexion,* he thought dreamily.

Step by step, Hilma and Tumbo maneuvered their way around postcard stands and waiters with trays of globby shadow-food samples.

"The Tower Obscura is right in the city center, as you may have noticed," Hilma said as she pushed away a plate of free samples. "Thankfully we only have a few more blocks to go."

The trio squeezed their way through the crowd, enduring the shove of shadow shoulders and oversized shadow handbags. At last, Hilma put her equipment down beside two thick glass doors. Panting, she announced, "We have arrived."

So distracted by this flood of new emotions, Tumbo
hadn't had a chance to look up. But he did now.

"My daisies, *that* is tall."

"Didn't I tell you?" said Earl. "We are in for a treat."

Tumbo squinted. "I can't make out where it ends."

The top of the teetering Tower Obscura was hidden in the clouds above. Tumbo marveled at the number of blocks needed to achieve this feat of a structure. His eyes traced the different forms up into the sky. Coming from a block closest to the cloud line, Tumbo swore he heard... rumbling. "What is that? Do you hear that, Hilma? That noise?"

"Don't worry Tumbo, I'm sure it just came from Dr. Strata's office. I forgot to mention, she's a cloud therapist. That's why the office we're going to is up so high. Sometimes her sessions get a little... stormy." Hilma chuckled.

Tumbo's love-drunk eyes sobered instantly into sheer panic. The last time he'd had a run-in with a thundercloud, his life had been flipped on its now not-so-curly head.

Hilma pushed open the heavy glass doors, and they entered the stone lobby of the Tower Obscura. She led them to a circular reception desk in the middle of the room. Aside from the well-dressed receptionist behind the counter, the lobby was empty. Tumbo stared at the vaulted ceiling above them, where an enormous mural had been painted—of thunderclouds.

"My name is Hilma Bristle, I have a four o'clock portraiture appointment with Dr. Strata. My apprentice, um, Tom, will be shadowing me this session." Hilma gave Tumbo a little wink.

The receptionist nodded. "Not a problem, Ms. Bristle. Dr. Strata will be ready for you shortly. Take the elevator on your left to floor 105 and make yourself comfortable." He slid two square cards across the counter to them. "If you could write your names on these IDs and clip them on for me, you'll be all set."

Tumbo took a marker from the desk and began to write out his name on the card, T...U—Hilma gave him a swift nudge. He immediately closed the top of the U, and followed it with an M.

"Okay Tom," she said, smiling. "Are you ready for the ride of your life?"

CHAPTER TWENTY-ONE

✷ BIRD'S-EYE VIEW ✷

Just as Hilma had told them, the Tower Obscura's elevator was made of glass. As Tumbo stepped through the elevator's scissor gate, he was abruptly surrounded by the busy streets of the city center.

The best view in Umbraton, he thought.

Hilma clapped her hands together. "We get a view of the city the whole way up!"

Tumbo swallowed.

"I hope you're not afraid of heights," Hilma said.

His stomach turned. *Heights are fine, just not thunderclouds,* he thought.

"May I have the honor of pushing the button?" said Earl.

Tumbo had never imagined a ring could be so excitable. He reached out his left hand, and, making a fist, bumped Earl into the dark button with the number 105 engraved into it.

"My dear Tumbo, would you also mind holding me up to the window so I can observe?"

With a small jolt, the elevator began to rise. It moved slowly at first but gained speed as it ascended. The walls of the surrounding buildings flew past, and within seconds they were above the rooftops of Umbraton, soaring toward the clouds.

Earl "oohed" and "aahed" as the city stretched out before them. Hilma pressed her fingertips to the glass and gazed thoughtfully into the horizon. Tumbo wiped a sweaty palm on his coat jacket; he felt like his stomach was trying to crawl out of his mouth. He didn't know what to be more nervous about—these new feelings for Hilma, or those old feelings for thunderclouds.

"Hilma, do you think there could really be a thundercloud in Dr. Strata's office?" Tumbo could feel his brow beginning to perspire.

Earl cooed as a lost balloon floated gracefully into the air.

"Maybe. But right now, let's not worry about a silly old thundercloud. Have a look at this spectacular view!" Hilma gave a jaunty smile. "Get your eyes out of the future, Tumbo. The present is more beautiful." She nudged his arm again with her shadow elbow. Tumbo couldn't help but smile.

Outside, a flock of gray birds flapped past the elevator window. Tumbo watched them go by. They seemed so sure of themselves, knowing exactly where to go and how to get there.

"I wish I could be one of those birds," Tumbo whispered.

Hilma laughed, "Good thing you're no wish-granter anymore Tumbo, or that may have come true faster than you'd be ready for it!"

Tumbo let out a small laugh, trying to hide his nerves.

Hilma patted his hand and looked at him in earnest. "I promise you Tumbo, a day will come when things don't feel so uncertain."

He stared at the birds gliding into the distance and remembered what it had felt like to fly out of Dog's mouth. How the cold air had prickled his cheeks and cleaned the spit from his face. He tried to imagine what it would be like to travel through the clouds on his own terms, instead of being hurled through them by someone else. His arms rose outward in a mock flutter. He looked hard into the horizon and pretended he knew where he wanted to fly. He tried to enjoy the flight, looking at the other birds who were with him on his journey, or rather, on *their* journey.

A bell chimed, and the elevator lurched to a halt. Floor 105. The black metal doors opened, and Hilma pulled aside the scissor gate.

"Adieu, adieu..." Earl said to the view outside the window. "Till we meet again, on the way down."

Tumbo shook his head, suddenly remembering he wasn't a bird en route to the horizon. The trio stepped out of their little glass cage and entered the waiting room. A patterned carpet covered the floor, and two rows of cushioned seats lined the walls. At the far end of the room stood a carved wooden door with a sign hanging from its handle. Tumbo squinted to make out what it said: *Thundercloud session in progress. Please take a seat.*

CHAPTER TWENTY-TWO

✳ CLOUD'S-EYE VIEW ✳

Inside Dr. Strata's office, Gerald the thundercloud hovered nervously over a velvet chaise lounge. Dr. Strata spoke from across the room, her voice was icy but gentle.

"If you need to let it out, Gerald, feel free to rain anytime you have the urge. But please, do refrain from using your lightning like you did in our last session."

Gerald drifted back and forth above the sofa. "Oh Doc, how I can possibly live with the knowledge of what I've done?! I know you said it was an accident— that it was self-defense—but I still don't think that's an excuse for... murder!!" Gerald burst into showers.

"You are a good cloud, Gerald. But if you ever want to ascend from this state and return to the stratosphere, you'll have to learn to love yourself—even when you make mistakes."

Dr. Strata sat behind a large desk, her wispy arms folded patiently on top of its sleek marble surface.

"Forgive myself for a mistake as serious as murder?!" Gerald's voice rattled the windows.

"I want to remind you that no cloud has come forward about a disappearance. It could be that in your fear you may have seen something that wasn't there." Dr. Strata picked up her pen. "Let's once more go over what you remember from that day."

"I know what I saw," Gerald grumbled. "I was over a field right outside of Terra Floss. A puffy white cumulus flew at me from below. I told them to stop or else—but they kept rushing towards me and I just... acted on impulse—shot them right through with a

lightning bolt. The next thing I knew—POOF! There was nothing left of them. Only a strange bald creature in a little green suit lying below."

"And were you able to talk to that strange bald creature?" Dr. Strata asked.

"*That* kind of creature?" Gerald puffed. "*Those* creatures don't listen to clouds in the Land of Light— they rarely even acknowledge us as beings! Besides, it made such an alarming sound as it lay there that I quickly blew away in fright."

Dr. Strata nodded, taking in some air. "Well, you have already reported the incident to the cloud authorities. Until you hear back from them, I would like to enroll you immediately in my seven-step course, *Self-love into the Stratosphere.*"

Dr. Strata took out a prescription form from her desk drawer. "Remember, my office is high enough to reach a border between Shadowland and the Land of Light. My clients are both shadow clouds and Land of Light clouds like yourself. I have met some clouds from the LOL who've gotten stuck in Shadowland, Gerald, and vice versa. Try not to let yourself get too weighed down by this, or you could sink into the depths of Shadowland and be trapped there... forever."

Gerald gasped.

"For that reason, I advise you to take my course as soon as possible." She waved one of her wispy arms, wrote out the prescription, and stamped it with a loud KA-CHING!

CHAPTER TWENTY-THREE

✳ LOOK OUT ✳

Tumbo paced the length of the waiting room. "Why don't you sit down and relax, Tumbo?" Hilma smiled. "You're going to wear the carpet through if you keep marching around like that."

Tumbo sat down in a chair across the room, but his fingers continued to drum themselves into the armrests.

"Excuse me, Tumbo," said Earl, who felt he was on a roller coaster with each anxious tap. "Could you tell us what's going on in that crystal-ball head of yours?"

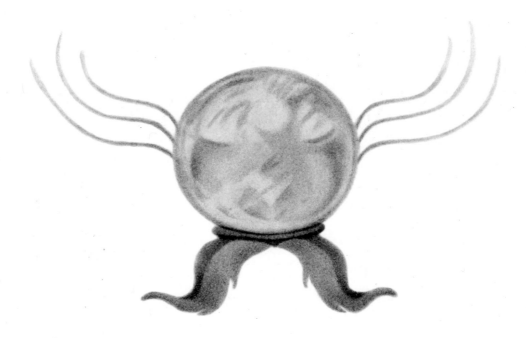

Tumbo blinked. *Going on in my head?* he thought. A lightning bolt blitzed behind his eyelids. A flash, and he could once again feel his tender scalp and smell the faint aroma of burnt hair. *Why did I come to this tower? A delightful elevator ride isn't going to get me out of Shadowland, and the last thing I need is to have my remaining hairs sizzled away by another treacherous thundercloud.*

"Whatever it is you are afraid of in there," said Earl, still bouncing, "well, as us diamonds like to say, the best way to face your fears is with a clear crown and an open pavilion."

Tumbo raised an eyebrow. Earl clarified, "A pavilion is our word for a heart."

Tumbo pursed his lips, *Earl could be right.* He clasped his fingers—squeezing Earl—to quiet them, and closed his eyes. He tried to clear his mind of thunderclouds... he imagined the moment Hilma had winked at him back in her apartment. The moment he'd looked at the portrait she'd painted and seen himself through *her* eyes. But the dark shadow of a cloud crept in through the side of his imagination. Tumbo's eyes shot open.

"You know, Tumbo?" said Hilma, "three floors up from here, on the very top of the Tower Obscura there's an observation deck. Why don't you and Earl wait up there while I'm painting Dr. Strata's portrait? Looking out over the horizon always helps to calm me down when I'm nervous. Maybe it will do the same for you."

Hilma rose and beckoned for him to follow. She pushed a big button next to the elevator door, and the mechanism inside the shaft began to whirr.

Hilma put a hand on his shoulder. "Remember what matters is who you *are*... and *I* think you are full of spark, Tumbo."

Tumbo's heart was as jittery as a jumping bean. *No one has ever seen me like she sees me,* he thought.

The elevator slid open with a sharp *ding!*, and Tumbo and Earl entered, closing the scissor gate behind them. Tumbo's body quaked: this time, not from the thought of a thundercloud.

"Hilma," he stammered, "there's something I need to tell you..."

Hilma raised a brow. Earl, being extra-sensitive to heartbreak, feared he could see where this was going.

Tumbo continued. "I think I may have... I think I may have feelings for y—"

Earl couldn't take it. To be part of yet *another* rejection?! He built up all the energy possible in his little pavilion and attempted to thrust himself, and Tumbo's hand, towards the "Close door" button.

The finger that Earl was wrapped around barely moved a wiggle.

Out from Tumbo came the finishing "—ou." The completed sentence floated in the air between them. *I have feelings for you.*

Hilma's other brow joined the first, raising way up high on her shadow forehead. Earl gritted his teeth.

But then, Hilma's brows came back down to their resting position. "Dearest Tumbo," she said, her shadow arm reaching through the scissor gate to rest on his shoulder, "I am so happy to hear you are having feelings other than doubt and shame. I have feelings of my own, but they want to stay here in Shadowland, and I believe *your* feelings belong back in the Land of Light."

Tumbo bowed his head. Earl held his breath.

Tumbo's heart had sunk down into his stomach, and he could feel Earl quaking. He searched deep into his pavilion for the right words to say. He raised his head and looked into Hilma's dark eyes. "Thank you, Hilma Bristle," he said, "thank you for seeing something in me that I couldn't see by myself. I am lucky that even when I don't know who I am or where I belong, I found those to show me a way to be. Even if they can't be with me."

Hilma smiled and gave a little wink.

Earl looked back and forth from Tumbo to Hilma. Everything was okay. He exhaled, astounded that not every rejection had to end in tragedy.

As if sensing this was a good note on which to leave, the elevator door jostled into action and began sliding closed. Hilma waved a goodbye. Tumbo could hear the handle of Dr. Strata's office open with a clack.

"Ms. Bristle, I'm ready for you now," said a crystalline voice. "See you next week, Gerald. You may take the elevator up to the very top floor to exit."

The elevator door sealed closed and the car rattled upwards. *Go up to exit?* Tumbo thought. *That's a strange way to leave a building.*

After a few moments, Tumbo and Earl emerged onto the rooftop. Its surface was made up of many rough stones all cemented together. They walked over to the edge, where there was a wall low enough to see over, but high enough not to fall over.

A strong wind blew.

Tumbo closed his eyes and took a deep breath. He tried to exhale the thunderclouds that filled his head and the sweet sadness of Hilma's response to his confession. He inhaled once more and decided to breath beyond all that and look on the bright side. He opened his eyes.

"Well, at least I don't have to worry about my hair getting messy," said Tumbo.

"Can we just forget about hair for a moment?!" Earl

yelled over the wind. "Now put your hands up onto this wall so I can take in this magnificent view!"

Tumbo laughed and followed orders. They took in the grayness of Umbraton together. "I'm happy to have you as my ring, Earl." Tumbo smiled. "Blustering buttercups, maybe it *is* okay to stay lost here in Shadowland, with friends like you and Hil—"

The elevator door dinged back open. Tumbo turned around quickly to see who could be coming out. His heartbeat quickened. Something large and gray was puffing its way through the scissor gate.

CHAPTER TWENTY-FOUR

✳ SEEING FULL SPECTRUM ✳

Tumbo stood as still as the stones under his feet. He faced the elevator door with his arms at his sides and his shoulders thrown back.

Gerald squeezed himself free from the gate. "Oh... hello," he said, clearly surprised to find someone out on the rooftop.

Tumbo held his breath. He repeated Earl and Hilma's words in his head. *A clear crown and an open pavilion... you are full of spark...*

✳

Gerald remained hovering in front of the now closed elevator door. He peered at Tumbo. "Pardon me for staring, but your form looks very familiar to me. Though most of my encounters are with clouds, and you certainly are no *cloud* I've ever met."

It couldn't be, thought Tumbo. *Dandelions above, out of all the thunderclouds to run into!* He sighed and repeated to himself, *I am full of spark.*

Tumbo smoothed his coattails. "Is it possible that you float around the fields of Terra Floss from time to time?" His voice quaked.

Gerald bobbed, speechless. He inspected Tumbo up and down. *That hairless head and that little suit...*

"It can't be!" Gerald squinted. "The bald creature from the field?! But that was a world away from here!"

Tumbo cleared his throat, but his first few words still came out as a squeak.

"You, Thundercloud, burned my hair away." He held back a tear. "You took away everything I have ever worked for. Why did you do it?" Tumbo pointed a shaking finger at his naked gray dome. "My beautiful white curls, what did they ever do to you?" Earl gasped.

"Curls?" said Gerald. "White ... *curls?*" Gerald replayed the traumatic event in his mind. *That puffy cloud had been floating so low to the ground.*

"Hold on a bluster, that white puffy cloud was... you? Does this mean I *didn't* murder a cloud after all?" he sputtered.

"Murder a *cloud*? Is that even–" Tumbo was interrupted by Gerald swirling into the sky.

"Oh holy vapors!" Gerald shouted in jubilation. He looked at the prescription for the seven-step course Dr. Strata had given him. "Seems like I won't be needing *this* anymore!"

Tumbo put his hands on his hips, his voice hot with frustration. "Well, you sure did *kill* my hopes and dreams, Thundercloud!" he yelled.

Gerald lowered himself down sheepishly.

"Oh dear... I *am* very sorry to hear that. At the time, I had mistaken you and your curls for a cloud bully coming to tease me. I was mocked so badly at school that I overreacted when I saw your puffy hair." Gerald floated to the side, afraid to ask the question. "Was it my lightning bolt that brought you here to Shadowland?"

Tumbo nodded.

"Was it because of my lightning bolt that you made that terrifying sound while you were lying there in that field?"

Tumbo nodded again.

Gerald looked at the prescription. "Maybe Dr. Strata's course would still be a good idea, even if I'm not a murderer."

Tumbo crumpled, tears welling behind his eyes.

Gerald hovered towards him. "Oh, can you ever forgive me, little bald creature?"

Tumbo rolled his eyes. He wanted to say, *Roses no! Of course not! How can I forgive someone who took my life away!* But he was having trouble staying angry at such a clearly sensitive cloud. He looked at Earl. He thought about what Hilma had said—that he could discover who *he* really wanted to be now that his curls had been taken away. *A clear crown and an open pavilion.*

"I forgive you, Thundercloud."

As the words left his lips, Tumbo felt something inside of him let go. He put his hand to his chest. It felt lighter, like a bird trapped in his ribcage had broken free.

"T-Tumbo?" Earl stammered. "I don't want to alarm you, but... you're leaking."

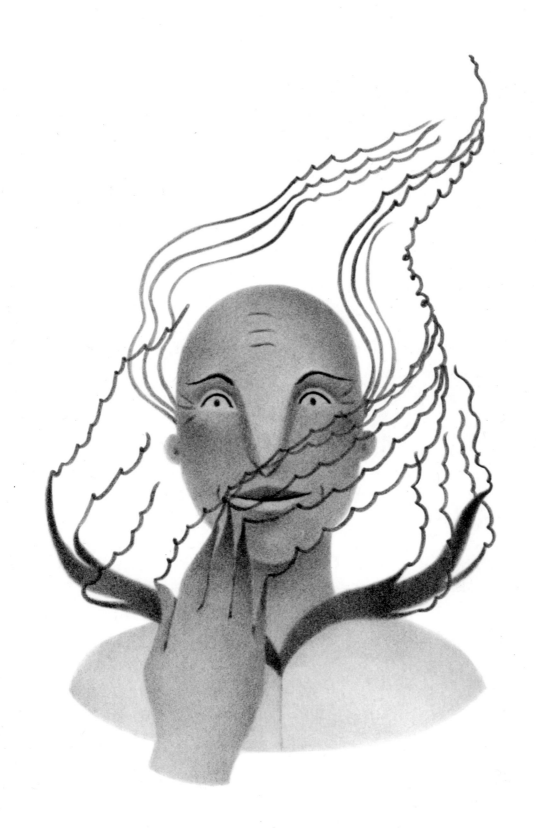

Tumbo raised a hand to his face. And indeed, he was. The grayness he had been made of since becoming a shadow was beginning to stream out through his fingertips.

"Ah, so I am," he whispered, spellbound.

Faster and faster the grayness poured from him, and all he could do was stand and watch. It whirled around his legs and up over his head, until his body was completely enveloped in a dark cloud of smoke.

Gerald, terrified, still hovered in front of the elevator.

"Little creature?!" he shouted, "Oh, I hope I haven't caused you harm yet *again*!"

Tumbo was too bewildered to reply. He stared at the last puffs of gray exiting from his pinky finger. He held his hands out in front of him, turning them from back to front. His body was translucent. The feelings of shame and doubt, that had brought him here to Shadowland, were gone.

Tumbo sensed a tingling in the crown of his head.

"Earl," he said, "*What* is happening to me?"

Memories appeared before his minds-eye, as real as if they were being projected out onto the smoke around him. *But these are new memories,* he thought.

He saw Jerry from The Center and remembered how he felt when she said she could find him a job. He saw Bonnie who had kept him from misdirecting his bitterness, and Dalinda who had helped him get up. There was Dog and the dandelion seed, reminding him of who he had been, and the lightbulbs who showed him who he could become.

"Whoa there!" he heard Gerald yelp from outside the smoke. "Be careful with that light!"

Tumbo looked down and saw, to his astonishment, that his breast was glowing. Filling the empty space of his body, warm energy expanded outwards from his core. It melted its way down through his legs and out through his arms like molten gold.

"Tumbo, you're doing it, old sprout!" Earl cried out.

Tumbo's eyes sparked. He concentrated on the new thoughts that entered his mind. There was finding food on his own in the gutters of Umbraton, and there was receiving the *gift* of food from Hilma, his rescuer. Oh,

Hilma. *The purpose of the journey isn't about who you will be, it's about who you are.*

Tumbo's body was radiating. "So *this* is delight," he whispered.

He held Earl up with a grin. "I *am* full of spark! Just like Hilma told me!" His eyes *flared*. Earl gasped.

The light shot from Tumbo like a beacon, directly into Earl. Trapped inside Earl's pavilion, the beam bounced around inside him, from facet to facet, from crown to tip. And then—like a scrambled egg too big for the pan, it broke out through the chip on Earl's shoulder and burst into the sky, reemerging into Shadowland in the form of a rainbow flying up through the dark clouds.

Tumbo laughed with exuberance, calling, "You were right, Dalinda, I'll know it when I feel it!"

He let the light flood through him. The brighter he shone, the brighter Earl's rainbow became.

"Tumbo, I think it is time for us to climb," Earl said with a sparkle. Tumbo grinned. He turned to Gerald, who was hovering, awestruck, by the ledge of the Tower Obscura.

"If I hadn't lost my curls, I never would have been able to choose who I am or who I want to be." Tumbo beamed. "I am TUMBO. I love to dance, I love to tell stories, and I even sort of love eating bitter shadow food. I can still make dreams come true, with or without my hair. Someday I may change, but that will be another chance to know myself better." Tumbo made a deep bow. "And for that, you have my deepest thanks, Thundercloud."

Gerald puffed with pride. "Please, call me Gerald."

"I hope we meet again someday, back in the Land of Light." Tumbo turned, and with one glimmering hand over the other, he pulled himself up the rainbow, and out of Shadowland.

CHAPTER TWENTY-FIVE

✳ LOL ✳

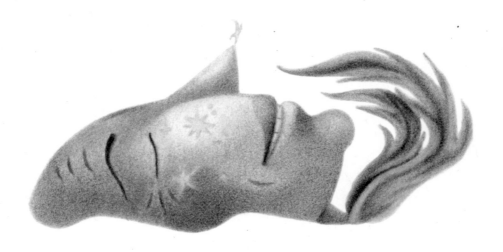

Light filtered through Tumbo's closed eyelids in splashes of pink and gold. He smiled, taking in a deep breath of cool air. The pitter-patter of something cold and wet fell gently onto his cheeks. He pulled up a hand to wipe it away and found that he could barely bend his elbow.

Has my body ever felt so stiff? He grasped at the ground, fluffy and freezing. Tumbo's eyes popped open. He was surrounded by snowy white. He sat up with a start.

The snow that had been covering him flew away like a blanket tossed aside after oversleeping.

"Have I been laying here in this same field since late summer?" he panted. "It can't be! But Shadowland... and—Earl!!!"

Tumbo picked his left hand up out of the snow. He let out a sigh of relief. There, sitting proudly on his finger, was the largest diamond ring he had ever seen. Earl was perfect in every way, except for that little chip on his shoulder.

"Oh Earl, I can't say how glad I am to see you."

Earl didn't reply.

"I didn't know you could be so quiet," Tumbo chuckled. "Hello?" He gave Earl a tap. Still, nothing. Earl was silent as a gemstone, but he did give a momentary sparkle.

Tumbo nodded solemnly. "I forgot how different things are in the LOL." He stood up and walked to his favorite birch tree, sitting down in a pile of snow at the base of her trunk… "Or *its* trunk, I suppose," Tumbo whispered. He watched the snow fall over the field, listening to the soft crackle the flakes made when they hit the ground.

"I am so glad to be back here," he whispered, giving the tree roots a pat. Tumbo rubbed his face. His fingers stopped abruptly in the space between his eyebrows. On what had once been smooth skin, he could now feel a slight vertical crease running up toward the top of his head.

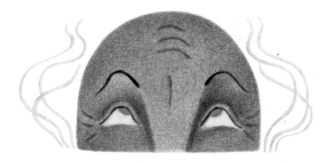

"Ah, my first not-so-happy wrinkle," Tumbo said. He looked down at Earl. "I'll wear it like that chip on your shoulder Earl—a keepsake from my first real adventure. I did go through a lot to get it after all." Tumbo looked up into the branches of the birch, half expecting to see Dalinda curled up within them.

"Flowers above, Dalinda!" he cried. "I nearly forgot about my promise!"

Tumbo closed his eyes and pursed his lips.

"All right, then," he said, taking a deep breath. In all his years of training, Tumbo had never actually granted a wish before. He rose to his feet, then up onto his tiptoes. Like beginning a pirouette, he brought his arms up to his middle and swiftly swung the right one up to the crown of his head. His hand paused, grasping one of his curly white hairs. With a light PLUCK, he snatched it out like a dandelion seed and brought it to his chest. He felt Dalinda's wish with his pavilion.

I wish to have my own story, she'd said.

He gave the wish time to travel through his fingertips and into the hair. Then, Tumbo brought the hair to his lips and blew. It somersaulted its way up into the sky and disappeared.

Watching its ascent, Tumbo remembered all the beings he had met in Shadowland, everyone who'd help him through.

They may not have asked for a wish directly, he thought, *but I feel they asked in their own way.*

Tumbo remained on pointed toe, and, bringing his arms back up to his waist, he repeated the wish-granting ceremony for Bonnie, for Gerald, for the lightbulbs at RCSC, and even for Dog himself.

One last little hair stood by its lonesome.

"This one is for me," he said. Plucking it out, Tumbo took a deep breath and prepared to recite his final wish. He hesitated, looking down at the curly hair between his fingertips, freshly picked and ready to emerge into the world. Tumbo let out a knowing sigh and smiled. "Or maybe you would like to make your own choice about who you want to be," Tumbo said to the hair. Cupping it gently in his hands, Tumbo brought the hair to his lips and blew it away into the wind without a word.

Up in the sky, the sun was beginning its descent, and Tumbo knew it was finally time to walk back to the city of Terra Floss. He put his left foot forward, then his right. Each footfall sank into the snow with a satisfying crunch. He still strode with the gracefulness of his years of training, but now his gait bore the slight wobble of experience.

At the edge of the field, Tumbo looked back, his gaze drifting into the clouds.

Dazzling daisies, was there something up there? He squinted. High above in the stratosphere was a long and slinking creature dancing on the cloud tops. Her ice-crystal scales sparkled pink in the setting sun.

Tumbo smiled. "It seems you have begun your own story," he whispered to Dalinda, and perhaps to himself as well.

Tumbo turned around. As he walked the frostbitten path that led back to Terra Floss, he didn't think about his parents' disappointment, or if the Flossians would point and laugh when they saw him. Nor did he think about what he would do in the future. Instead, Tumbo gave Earl a wink and continued across the field, enjoying the way the snow glittered as it danced along his footsteps.

✳

Acknowledgments

It takes a village to write a book. (At least if you are like me.) I would like to give a thank you deeper than the deepest depths of Shadowland to everyone who has read, commented, and wrangled this manuscript into what it became in the end. Something that is maybe still not perfect, but lightyears better than what it would have been were it not for all of your feedback, guidance, and inspiration.

A special thank you to my husband Marcos Weiss for always being there to listen and give me feedback and encouragement throughout this entire journey. To my monthly writing critique group: Keth Pryke, Chuck McDaniel, Heather Rising, Michaela Bellach, and Craig Barfoot for teaching me how to be a better writer and pushing me on plot and character. Thank you to Jessica Miller and her fiction writing class. To the two incredible people, Emily Pollak and Laureen Mahler, who edited this manuscript. I am beyond grateful for your unprecedented dedication and help with this book. Thank you to my publishers Roy Freeman and Marc Schmuziger for believing in this story even when it was only my overly-enthusiastic plot summary, before it was even written. To my good friend Jeana Bellows for helping me find a way out of Shadowland. To my mom Deb Samuels for her edits and plot critiques. To my brother Kai Samuels-Davis for giving me confidence. And to my dad Jim Davis, for reading me so many of the books that inspired me to write this one.

Last but not least, to this doodle I drew on
a chalkboard almost a decade ago. Thank you
for giving me the idea for this story. Maybe
it's finally time to wipe the slate clean. :)